OVERSTAYING

Art on cover © 2022 by Lucie Kohler
Sur la plage abandonnée
A4 29.7 x 21cm, pencils on paper

The publisher wishes to thank David Ehmcke and Natasha Muhametzyanova.

ISBN: 978-1-948980-19-7

Library of Congress Cataloging-in-Publication Data available upon request

Design and composition by Danielle Dutton
Printed on permanent, durable, acid-free recycled paper in the United States of America

Dorothy, a publishing project books are distributed to the trade by New York Review Books

Dorothy, a publishing project | St. Louis, MO
DOROTHYPROJECT.COM

OVERSTAYING

— ARIANE KOCH —

Translated by Damion Searls

DOROTHY, A PUBLISHING PROJECT

THE VISITOR SAT AT THE TABLE eating his little tangerine slices. Whenever things are excessively small, I can't help but raise my eyebrows and put my hand on my heart, or at least where I presume my heart is. No one has ever had trouble making me stop misbehaving, all they had to do was offer me something miniature.

The visitor is delicate, so very delicate that he practically wafts apart. At first I didn't notice, because he's very good at hiding it. Anyone as delicate as the visitor is in grave danger. How easily he might end up in the clutches of some crazy person. My great-grandfather, for instance, was a well-known cult leader. Alas I was not so fortunate as to ever have met him personally. All I have of him is a single photograph showing him at a writing desk, his hair in a severe part, gaze aimed into a visionary future. I also find it fascinating that the sermons he gave were apparently improvised: he would let the Holy Scripture drop onto the pulpit, the beneficent hand of the Lord would make the book fall open at a choice passage, and he would thereby be presented with the subject of his sermon.

My great-grandfather might have put it thus: You have to trust the page that the Holy Book opens to when it falls, and anyway one is merely the servant of the Lord, there is nothing to do but carry out His will.

Next to the small town where I have come to rest, as if in a sarcophagus, there is a large mountain, rather like a pyramid, but not, like the actual wonder of the world, able to be sightseen from within, and furthermore capped with snow. One can, if one truly wants to, climb it. I personally refrain—by now the view's been ruined for me and it's no longer possible to see as far as I would like. I prefer to remain at the mountain's feet. Sometimes the mountain's shadow scares me.

I know everyone in this town but mostly act like I don't know anyone. Something or other has happened to me on practically every streetcorner by now; various temporal strata are superimposed. There's always quite a bustling crowd in the Roundel Bar, which is located right near my house; it was originally supposed to be open for only a hundred days, but that hundred has turned into thousands. The waiter changes every week, and each one is more appalling than the last, but they all keep their hair tied up tight on their heads, and even aside from that it's safe to say there has never been anything interesting to see there. I always knew that I was ungrateful. My parents prophesied it early on, and I never denied it.

The visitor was uncharted territory. He materialized from the void. He got off the train, walked down the platform swinging his suitcases, and our gazes met. It's not entirely clear to me whether the insane idea to come here was his own. I was standing on the other side of the platform, contemplating departure, or at least wandering around the train station trying to get an overview of all the destinations I might possibly travel to. But I've never set foot on a train.

I can't deny it: the visitor seemed familiar the first time I stared at him through the gold-rimmed lenses of my glasses—or was it he, standing on the other side of the platform, who fixed his eyes warmly on me through the lenses of his, while we both knew we'd come from opposite directions and so would travel onward in opposite directions too, the next day or at the very latest the day after? It was this look from the visitor that burned into my mind and that I've been seeking in the looks of other people ever since that moment, and sometimes I find it, today it came from the moderator of a philosophical panel discussion on TV and was aimed at a young French writer.

They said on the radio that the animals in the zoo aren't used to human beings anymore and take flight at the slightest human movement. Especially the flamingoes. The image of people drifting through the zoo while the animals take off for the great wide open is one I find pleasing.

Then came an interview with the head of tourism for the small town (into which I was involuntarily born and where I do not plan to die); he wanted to boost tourism by presenting the little town as a major metropolis. This statement struck me as so nonsensical that I didn't know what to do with myself. At the Roundel, large flakes from a croissant had been scattered across the bar with its thin plastic coating of fake marble. They glittered gold in the sun. The mountain, the head of tourism went on, was a great attraction already, of course, but the aerial tramway was tottering, the cable cars swinging ominously— renovations were urgently needed.

I didn't make a habit of going to the bar in the middle of the day, but the recent appearance of the visitor had driven me out of the house that morning to take up the search for him.

Outside, people I was only able to perceive as silhouettes walked up and down the streets. I observed a mother resignedly pulling her berserk child by the hand. Sitting at the marble bar, one leg crossed over the other, I imagined that only teeny-tiny people lived in this small town, riding around on teeny-tiny bicycles and tossing down ristrettos from teeny-tiny coffee cups. I had no problem picking up the entire Roundel Bar in my hand, turning it around, and examining it from all sides, while the people sitting on the barstools shrieked and tried to hold on; their teeny-tiny drinks had already fallen, plummeted, and landed on my jeans as little drops. The people, now hanging on for dear life, stared at me with wide minuscule eyes as I tore the Roundel in half down the middle, like a donut. I imagined the small town getting smaller and smaller, shrinking down to a tiny point—I alone remained large, so I no longer fit in it. Then it occurred to me that this was already the situation.

The radio was broadcasting a report about the increasing wave of violence against caregivers. The bartender turned the radio down, and the voices drifted away.

People are lying under awnings, sometimes in sleeping bags, sometimes in tents, sometimes in sleeping bags in tents. They mostly keep their luggage stored in holes in the street covered with trap doors. How many times have I seen them crawling out from these holes tugging shapeless pieces of luggage behind them. The people have taken on the color of the buildings they sleep in front of—gray, like the sidewalks—while their tents and sleeping bags light up the whole town with their neon colors. In winter there is a team of workers in orange protective vests who go looking for people without fixed domiciles and bring them groceries and occasionally wet wipes.

There is one woman I've noticed several times. During the day her clothes are irreproachable—she wears a light-gray coat and hurries down the street as though going to work. When night falls she lies down in her sleeping bag wearing tattered sweatpants and stares out dully, right into my face, and I in return look into her face whenever I'm crossing the street back from the Roundel Bar to my house or vice versa. We don't say anything, we just share this look.

At the end of the street, where the woman sometimes sets up her temporary sleeping quarters, there's a furniture store that specializes in sofas. The furniture store really might as well call itself a sofa store, there are so many sofas crammed next to one another in the shop windows. It has extended business hours until late in the evening so that people with jobs can look for their sofas too. Most often it's couples who go in, try out sitting on sofa after sofa, and leave again with faces stunned by their purchase. Soon, very soon, the mountain of cotton will be delivered to them at home. Soon a moving truck will stop in front of their house. Soon two guys will heave a mountain of cotton out of the truck and carry it up the stairs, bumping it into everything along the way. Soon the mountain of cotton will be in the couple's apartment, and the couple will sit down upon it in disbelief and sink into it.

I sometimes wish I had slightly less good eyesight. But then I might not have seen the visitor holding up coins foreign to him under the lights shining down onto the circular bar at the Roundel. We sat across from each other at a safe distance, sipping our respective beers and then our respective next beers for hours on end. One on one side of the roundel, the other on the other side. The sight line ran straight through the circle, connecting our two points and transfixing the center point, the waiter, who was shifting from one foot to the other. Perhaps it was not the first time, and also not the last time, that I drew such a line in the Roundel Bar. No one ever sleeps in this town anymore, most people sit at the bar, sip drinks from tin cups, and contemplate whom on which diagonal they might start up an affair with. I can often predict the future connecting lines of the people sitting there, the secants' points of intersection. When someone tries to approach me I generally move around the circle in the opposite direction so that we never converge, remaining a fixed distance away from each other. That is to say, I too receive mail from men every now and then in which I can read that they've seen me and, even though they don't know me, my smile, which they say they're certain was directed at them, has said yes. I can't with the best will in the world remember ever once having smiled.

The visitor walked around like a sticky strip of flypaper with insects stuck to it. He was clearly looking for a place to stay, although he seemed not to know it yet. He traipsed around outside the Roundel Bar, down the lanes, up the mountain.

Anyway, I felt a little uneasy.

I was suddenly seeing him everywhere, as though there was no one besides him, as though he would be wandering through the town swinging his luggage forever, examining forever the gap in the clouds that was growing ever larger, the moonlight breaking through it. Meanwhile his silhouette shimmered, silvery.

I put down my binoculars for a moment so that the image could burn itself onto my retina like lightning flashing in the night sky.

I have a big house even though it doesn't look that way from the outside. It's gigantic, though not as big as the mountain outlined so sharply against the light. I don't own my house, I only superintend it to make sure it doesn't fall apart. At some point my brothers and sisters will take over the house. At some point I will have to move out of my house, I will be driven out, namely when my brothers and sisters announce their desire to possess the house once more. They have the money to say that my house should belong to them. They might well become land barons and baronesses while I am the warden of a ruin. They will move into my house and renovate, convert, add onto, and turn it into a house different from the one it is now. Maybe it will be bigger and taller; it will definitely be more luxurious. It will definitely be painted a different color.

In general I feel that over the years this house has kept changing into a different house.

When my parents moved in here with me and my brothers and sisters, many years ago, I installed a little cable car line to the neighbors' house and exchanged letters with the neighbor child. Sometimes we also showed each other objects by holding them up to our window—a silent dialogue of things dancing back and forth behind the windowpane. For example, I saw a stuffed polar bear, then a pair of scissors. I answered with a stuffed donkey and some indefinable bramble I had manufactured in kindergarten. When I got older I cut the cord, which fell down on the hedge and turned into a trembling line running through the yards. I had a bad feeling that there was no real reason for me to have done that, yet contact with the neighbor child remained broken off for good.

The cats, too, came and went, were run over, got fat, got castrated. I remember Rambo, Caesar, and Napoleon. Now one, now the other ruled the yards, swaggering through the greenery with tail held high. There was constant warfare over territorial boundaries and the smell of cat piss filled the air; even my parents' efforts to make the cats go to the bathroom elsewhere—efforts consisting of scattering pepper—failed.

Now they're all dead. Their lives were spent in yards.

And I'm still here. Living like a tomb-keeper among things I don't own that are increasingly falling to pieces. Leaning too hard against the walls is not advisable. Stones fall out of the façade. The front yard is covered with leaves, and dirt, and snow.

If it were up to me I wouldn't need a house at all, no architecture of any sort, because I really don't know how to appreciate it. You could just stick something up and tell me it's a house and I'd believe it. I've never had an eye for architecture, despite living in the most outlandish house in the whole town. It's a real blind spot I have for masonry. The plaster has to fall off my façade at my feet before I even notice that there's plaster on my house. I see qua blindness straight through the masonry of the building to the people who live there. Picture something like a dollhouse with one of the walls missing.

I have an excellent memory for the people who live in a house, unlike for the house itself. Their coloration, their clothes, their way of walking down stairs or standing up from the table and turning on the stove. I must confess that I only rarely let other people into my house, and yet it is memories of them and their lives that blow as traces through the house's rooms and corridors. My parents may have left but their way of occupying architectural space remains.

My grandfather once built a dollhouse complete with electric lights, even light switches. When I used to go visit my grandparents it was one of my favorite pastimes to flick the teeny-tiny light switches on and off, illuminating the dollroom with teeny-tiny floorlamps and overhead lights complete with patterned lampshades, then darkening it again. I never touched the dolls. I remember that I left them lying in their wooden beds under the blankets—they needed their sleep. At some point the light switches broke; the fact is, my grandfather had nine other grandchildren besides me, who flicked the little switches in the dollhouse at least as obsessed with them as I was.

I wonder what makes people love little things so much. I fear it might have something to do with the fact that their offspring (children) are also little, and bigger people have to look after them or else they'll starve.

There are the people who want a house but don't have one and the people who have a house but don't want one. There are people with ugly houses and people with other overnighting options, for example a mobile home, tent, or sleeping bag. The boundaries between the various categories of domicile are fluid, like boundaries in general. But we might say that someone who temporarily lays claim to domestic lodgings that don't belong to them on the one hand steps across this fluid boundary and thus on the other hand may be termed a visitor.

I once had a friend who liked how I constantly started sentences with *on the one hand* and *on the other hand*, despite not using the terms correctly. Rather than communicating opposite views, I used them simply to tack on the same viewpoint again.

On the one hand a roundel is a military fortification, on the other hand a defensive structure from which one could observe the enemy from a safe distance, for instance through binoculars. If one were on the one hand not in the mood for the enemy or his approach, one could on the other hand shoot at him from the roundel with arrows. Anyone standing on the roundel would have a view over all his enemies or subjects, should he have any. On the roundel he could act like he did have such even if he didn't. It is also possible to add optional moats around the roundel. I would recommend a roundel to anyone who needs to want to feel bigger.

The waiter in the Roundel is acting exactly like he doesn't hear my beer order.

In the place where the visitor came from, he no longer is. In the place where he was, there is now only a non-him. In the place where the visitor no longer is, someone is dealing with a gap, an empty space, possibly a pulsating empty space. Someone finds him- or herself confronted with the visitor's absence. Someone is possibly baffled, possibly sad, possibly happy about it.

Everything the visitor might be too much of here, he is perhaps too little of somewhere else. Here there was nothing missing. Here no one was waiting for a visitor. Here there is everything to excess already.

Only the Roundel Bar is gradually falling apart. The golden kerchiefs tacked to the walls are increasingly coming loose; the people drinking along the ring of the bar, too, are getting wrinkles, first in the corners of their eyes, then in the corners of their mouths. Sooner or later their jowls will be hanging down into their beer foam. The Roundel Bar is turning more and more into a museum housing fossils. Sometimes I imagine wall text, glass cases, basins to put the fossils into: the artist with the walrus mustache; a woman with very long hair and a busy-looking face who likes to wear a dress that looks like fish scales; another woman with shorter hair whose drinks sometimes slip spectacularly out of her hands. Yes, even these fossils need a home.

The fact is, all my life I've longed to go away but then I've never left. The fact is, I've been thinking about leaving and talking about leaving my whole life long but I'm still here. I am the oldest fossil of all, and I hate this small town so much that I'll have my revenge on it by never actually leaving, even if I constantly act like I'm about to. I am the oldest fossil of all, and even if someone asked me on bended knee to leave here I would stay anyway.

Maybe the only one who has understood the difference between possibilities and actualities is the visitor. Maybe he never actually wanted to go anywhere at all, maybe he just wanted to stay where he was, all his life, but he has nevertheless managed to privilege the un-avoidable over the unwanted.

I thought I should tell the visitor that he should be proud of him-self for having understood something that a small town full of fossils is never, not for one single second, capable of understanding—not even when rooms are pressing down onto their skulls. I thought I might tell the visitor about my possible departure so that he could prognosticate its feasibility. Or maybe I hoped that, if I got closer to the visitor, a little of his having left would spill over onto me and flush me out of town like a giant wave. In short: I needed an expert.

Sometimes I think I shouldn't talk about leaving anymore because I've already talked about it too much. Not a day goes by that I don't talk about leaving; I never get tired of talking about it. I wonder if the only way it's possible to stay somewhere is if you constantly talk about leaving. Since someone who only talks about staying has really, on the inside, long since left already, right?

One can also stay with someone by leaving with him.

Everyone could go away and never stay anywhere.

Everyone could stay, and in fact could stay exactly where they are right now.

I slipped off the barstool, semicircled the bar, and stopped on the other side, next to the visitor, but I can't with the best will in the world provide an accurate calculation of my path, my half-circumference. It might have been two steps, it might have been a hundred. I thought I would die when I got there, or else the visitor would break into a dance that would make me laugh. I stood before him, the visitor, and he raised his bespectacled gaze and stared straight into my eyes so that I promptly fell into his shining pupils. His hairs, at the time still quite short, jutted out in hedgehog fashion. If only I'd known how much that stubble was capable of growing. The visitor didn't dance when I came up to him, he only asked: Do you want to have a baby? or maybe something else that he got from flipping through the last pages of a small, badly out-of-date dictionary. It didn't make me laugh. The waiter in his position at the center of the circle turned toward us, held out his arms with a beer affixed to each one, and put them down on the bar in front of us, where their wavering crowns of foam lapped in our direction.

The visitor was wearing a zipperless raincoat, a poncho of the kind I had only seen on children. I remembered that when you were wearing such a raincoat and tried to take it off there would be a moment when you staggered, unable to find the exit, i.e., openings for your head and arms, hence disorientedly flailed around until eventually at some point you made your way into the light. In any case, the visitor's extremities surged helplessly out of the rain cape's holes as he apparently waited for me to answer him in some way. So I said that my brothers and sisters would hate him. He nodded.

The outer limit of our time together was already hanging above the bar. It's too bad that we always miss the beginnings of things, while the ends of said things always hammer into our bodies. The last thing I thought before I fell into his clutches was that I had to be careful not to fall into his clutches.

I led him through the streets, completely off-leash, nonetheless he trotted docilely behind me, rain poncho aflutter. And suddenly the roads I had walked up and down a thousand times before were different. His gaze made things shrink or grow, made spatial perspectives and colors change like a chameleon's—my favorite animal by the way. Their feet are like soft forceps that they hold onto branches with, or not just hold onto, claw them tight. When they move it's only in slow motion while their eyes dance around like wild. I imagine that if I owned a chameleon it would sit on my shoulder and scare off passersby by flicking its tongue out every so often.

I pointed out the signs that themselves pointed in various directions one could choose among, as I would myself someday, I told the visitor. Hong Kong, Paris, Budapest. It seemed to me as though a cloud descended upon the visitor as his gaze drifted to the signs, but he only gave a friendly nod. One thing I liked about the visitor was that I never knew if he could actually understand me.

I pointed to the mountain, and he looked up at it, shielding his eyes from the sun, his brushy fingers throwing a delicate pattern of shadow onto his face. I looked down at him and asked myself why he was wearing such light shoes, practically sandals, under his rain jacket—which resembled, when I thought about it, a tent—especially with winter lurking around every corner.

I suddenly remembered one time when I had ventured outdoors

with my father in weather as cold as you could imagine—the ground was covered with ice—and how my father had unceremoniously stuck little knobs to his shoes and run off, while I, without suitable footwear, slid across the icy surfaces. We took a jog through the woods, he sure of foot and me right behind him flailing my arms, unable to control my balance. Not one single time did my father turn around to check on me; he seemed not to take any notice of my falling condition.

I said to the visitor: You know how you can go somewhere you've never been but still have the feeling you've already been there? As for me, no matter where I go, I'm always reminded of something I'm already familiar with. And so I sometimes feel really disappointed, about how our minds always seek out what's known in the unknown, instead of surrendering to the unknown.

The visitor smiled and made a triangle with his fingers, but I wasn't sure whether it was supposed to be a roof or a pyramid or if he was just stretching a little out of boredom. We walked into the shadow of the mountain and stopped in front of my house, the biggest house in the whole small town. At various times, I had considered putting a fence up around the house. Does it sound over the top to say I'd considered sirens to scare off cats?

I absolutely wasn't planning to take him in. I never intended to turn my oddity into duality. But it had been conveyed to me that taking in guests is a proper and civilized thing to do. Especially when they're loitering about and have no idea what to do with themselves. I myself certainly have lots of ideas about what to do with myself. My imagination downright bubbles over, and so I have enough to share with someone else, on special occasions, I thought.

There are two lions on guard in front of my house, both with jaws open wide, each resting a paw on a respective sphere, yet they did not scare off the visitor. I said to him: You're welcome to come stay with me but you'll have to bring your own mattress, unless you want to sleep on an air mattress that the air gradually leaks out of so that you're actually sleeping on the floor, but not directly on the floor, since I own a Persian carpet that someone forgot and left here once, but I don't mind if you use it, that is, lie on it, when you're in the mood for a sore neck.

And so the visitor hauled a mattress with a salmon-colored slipcover through the small town. I presume the lady in the light-gray overcoat loaned it to him. Now and then he put the mattress down on a park bench, took a short break, and stared up once again at the mountain, which peered back down, impassive as always, just like the passersby.

I hadn't been polite enough to help him carry his luggage. He managed it, but only puffing heavily, in a slightly bent posture, tipping either to the left or to the right. He made it up the stairs, step by step, scraping the walls of the hall, and finally moved into the room, which was square and stuffed with broken vacuum cleaners. The visitor put the mattress between the flapping vacuum cleaner nozzles that would quietly nuzzle up to him at night, something he did not yet expect.

I took in the visitor because I live in a house with ten rooms and reside in only nine of them, which is to say, I have an empty room. As a result I always used to get phone calls from interested parties, even though I had never advertised the room publicly. At some point I simply stopped answering the phone. The room got dusty, and I thought: I should repurpose it. Housepets could live there, or nomads. One time I even considered a butler. The room used to belong to someone who was permanently traveling, which I found convenient. At first they would regularly send me photos and postcards; later, I never heard from them again. The person's name is still affixed to the mailbox, but by now it's been bleached by the sun, blurred by the rain, and made illegible. My name, in contrast, remains wonderfully legible.

I've never actually known what kind of name it is that I was bequeathed. I never bothered to look it up, this name I was condemned to bear. Every now and then I run across namesakes in books, for instance a misogynist judge from around the turn of the century, an insane biologist specializing in parasites, or a company whose mission is to manufacture weapons and send them out into the world.

The visitor has a name too, of course. A really long one, in fact. But it's so long that one simply cannot remember it, no matter how hard one tries.

I find myself suddenly reminded of a story that the artist with the walrus mustache once shared from his barstool at the Roundel:

One day he'd gotten a phone call from a man who politely asked if he could be this artist's assistant for a couple weeks, at no cost, he just wanted to watch the artist at work. The artist hesitated a bit but then said yes. The assistant was happy and asked for the name of a hotel near where the artist lived. The artist at once invited the man to stay with him, since he lived in a very remote location and there were no hotels nearby. The assistant arrived the next day, but when the artist opened the door the new assistant had only a smallish plastic bag with him. He cheerfully went to the guestroom and wrapped himself up in the blanket on the bed, even though they'd agreed that he would bring his own sleeping bag. The artist was a little taken aback but then had to focus his attention once more on his three children, whom he was raising alone at the time.

The next day, the assistant had planned to get up at six in the morning to paint the sunrise but ended up stumbling downstairs at ten. The artist had set aside three omelettes for the visitor and offered them to him, who accepted them like it was the most natural thing in the world and ate them. While partaking of the omelettes, the assistant also expressed the wish to start painting now after all, except unfortunately he had no painting supplies with him. Then, to satisfy his guest's wishes, the artist cleared out a corner for him and offered him an easel and a canvas and paints. He started brushing away at the canvas at once, but soon expressed disappointment at there being no black among the offered paints. The artist explained to him that he would only rarely need any black, for a very particular reason. The assistant replied that he didn't care in the least about the reason, the artist should just hand over the black paint. The artist found the expensive deep-black paint, and the assistant squeezed it directly onto the canvas, the whole tube, and smeared it around with his hands.

I'm not sure, did I sleep at all during the first few days after he arrived? I only remember putting out a hand towel for him, which he grudgingly took in his claws. I remember him retrieving from his shapeless bag an item meant to constitute something edible, and putting it in my hand in exchange. I remember that I flinched when his brushfingers brushed against me because it reminded me of the time, many years ago, when a boy tried to hold my hand during a concert and I fainted. I remember how lying on the floor between all the people's legs felt really nice.

All my life people have criticized me for not touching them enough. I attract people, sure, but then it's hard to shake them off again. Everyone around me can just catapult away whole droves of people with little shakes of their hips, but I shake and shake mine as wildly as I can, and I can't get rid of anyone. They're more likely to burst out laughing than anything else when I break into my jiggling dance. Or maybe it's the jiggling dance that emboldens them to never want me to leave their side. Probably my jiggling dance is already the talk of the whole small town. Anyway, it's a good thing to never entirely stop jiggling, in other words, to preemptively shake even when there's not a single human soul as far as the eye can see.

I remember the first morning: The sleepless visitor got up, escaped into the open air, and ran a few laps, circling and sniffing the house. I prepared the culinary specialty of the house for him. He sat out on the balcony, even though it was ice cold, and gobbled down the egg dish. His eyes glittered strangely when he thanked me.

I remember he was talkative, that he felt my house reminded him of his father's house, which he would someday inherit, and which likewise had two little stone lions standing out front. I remember that I said my stone lions weren't little. The visitor went on with his excessively detailed description of his father's house, in a voice that was loud and gentle at once; his eyelids smoothly opened and closed, his head tilted back and forth. He described for me the driveway and the garden shed that was the first thing you saw when you drove up from the village street. The main building was situated behind a tree—a patient house, standing there on the hill and waiting for summer to come and give it a little sunlight. The visitor went on to say that he sometimes imagined what it would be like to live there, but actually he could never go back there again. His father was so lost that the whole environment around his father was equally lost. He then said that at first he couldn't believe lostness was contagious like that, and he was sorry but he couldn't say anything else at the moment about his father's lostness.

I said that maybe fathers are intrinsically lost creatures. My own father, for instance, never sought out other people's company. He hadn't, like the visitor's father, grown up in a house with a yard and lion statues; he and his three siblings had shared a small city apartment. He never had a room of his own, not even his own bed. He spent the nights in the living room on a foldout sofa, never knowing if it might not suddenly snap shut again, folding him up along with it. He was never alone as a child, and maybe that, I said, was the reason why he spent the rest of his life seeking anonymity, welcoming it, and avoiding sofas.

Sometimes I don't remember if I actually said that. Because the guest doesn't speak my language. Maybe we only thought we were reading each other's stories in each other's eyes. Maybe I was the one who saw forlornness twinkling in him. The ground outside was deep-frozen, as was time—nothing was moving as far as the eye could see, except the visitor gulping down his eggs.

In the nine rooms the visitor doesn't live in, crates with my name written on them have piled up over the years. I've packed some of them in advance for my departure. Since then I've forgotten what's in them, and when I occasionally get bored, I imagine their contents thus: giant floorlamps, a little dancing bear, a plastic gun. Sometimes I think they aren't my crates at all, just crates that someone wrote my name on so they wouldn't have to take them. Sometimes the contents are transformed into other things, like in a magic trick: all you need to do is wish hard enough.

The visitor wants to push the crates aside a little to give the room better light. The visitor was not supposed to bring any furniture, except for a mattress, but also was supposed to avoid touching my things as much as possible. He was supposed to pay rent but not put his name up on the mailbox. I don't care at all about furnishings, but I've always kept everything exactly how my parents left it, even though they're long gone. In practically fleet-footed fashion they left everything behind, while I stay stuck in this bog and have been condemned since that day to dwell in their leavings. My parents didn't seem to have a problem relinquishing their responsibility for these things, and for me. They might have just cleared out the house and sold it if it wasn't for me insisting that everything remain exactly how it used to be. My life has never been an especially great burden on my parents, but nor has it enriched them much. Possibly they were sometimes unable to conceal their disappointment about this.

If the house caught on fire, I wouldn't take anything with me, but I also wouldn't leave.

My reputation seems to have improved since the visitor has been occupying my house and my time. For example, there are neighbor children who never used to even glance at me, who now constantly kick soccer balls into my yard, supposedly by accident, so that they can knock on my front door and gawk at the visitor.

Every time this happens the visitor jumps up to offer them candy, and I don't prevent him. It's all the same to me whether or not he's planning to poison the neighbor children. They're all right, because they're small, but then again they're not that small; now that I think about it, they have chubby thighs.

The neighbor children suck on their exotic candies, still gawking, but they don't move from the front door. I contemplate availing myself of the broom, or the herd of spooky vacuum cleaner nozzles. The visitor beats me to it, though, by laughing and trying to hold the children's hands, at which they run back outside, shrieking.

My reputation seems to have risen so high that the head of tourism for the small town has a personal letter sent to me, sincerely thanking me for my efforts. He writes that helping one's fellow man is by no means something we can take for granted; there are plenty of single women squatting in gigantic, crumbling houses just waiting for death to come, although it often takes its time, and so the corridors in these houses grow dusty, each one painted its own specifically intuited color—

Look out! There are so-called conmen roaming the streets of the cities, ringing doorbells and talking the poor women and men living in those houses into buying nonsensical color combinations—and in those very motley-colored but unused corridors there are full-fledged dust balls lying around, so these cold-hearted women buy vacuum cleaner after vacuum cleaner, every last one of which collapses in the face of the immensity of these lumps of dust, so that whole collections of broken vacuum cleaners are left standing around in these people's houses, useless. We can only assume that these vacuum cleaner armies are increasingly getting into formation, yes, or in any case are increasingly up to some nefarious scheme, there's no way to be sure exactly what. At all events, he is extraordinarily pleased that I am making a significant contribution to the struggle against the out-of-control vacuum cleaner population explosion by billeting unhoused individuals with me. The community of those allergic to dust thanks me as well.

Occasionally when I find myself in the darkness of the bottomless pits of the world, I call up one or another of my friends and acquaintances to inform them how it's going for a member of a discriminated minority, and when I pull off an especially good description I receive in return deep admiration for my social and humanistic engagement, which I accept with pretend modesty and a fake cough. It is of the utmost importance that a visitor feel comfortable, I then say. That he feel taken in hand, floating along. Therefore it is never at any point appropriate to complain about the visitor's proclivities or seem to question his particular ways—no, it is all the more urgent to welcome and incorporate them affirmingly into one's daily routine, I pontificate into the telephone.

Meanwhile I think to myself: I will only very, very rarely let the visitor interact with other people. He should be my scientific experiment, mine alone. I need only feed him enough and make sure he knows that I am the mistress of this house. It's not even like he'd notice his scarf hanging out the bottom of his jacket in back like a tail, dragging along the floor.

The visitor is all alone with me, I think, before I drop into bed at night.

At first you still make an effort. You brush your teeth, you put the toilet seat down. At first you carry yourself as if you're just passing through and are soon to depart. At first you still behave like a civilized person whose parents have brought you up properly. I was never brought up properly. I had to bring myself up, from the very beginning, feed myself, all of that—except for the house, which was provided to me since I had no source of income of any kind. Still, I work all day. Sometimes I can't even say what I work on. It's not like I go looking for work to do, more like the other way around. Ever since the visitor has been here I've had my hands full, even though he's the one who looks after the housekeeping.

When he sits down at the table with a freshly made meal for himself, I want to try it. The visitor jumps up to set a place for me but I don't mind eating directly from his plate. The crema on the coffee he makes is also just perfect, in my opinion, which I convey to him to the extent of giving him a barely perceptible nod. The visitor doesn't even like coffee, he only dips his tongue quickly into the coffee cup and then scrunches his face into a grimace that almost makes me smile.

I took in the visitor because life had become boring, because filaments of dust were hanging from the walls, because *somebody* had to get rid of these filaments of dust, and because the vegetables were threatening to rot in the fridge. The visitor took it upon himself to take care of these matters like it was the most natural thing in the world. I let him clean all the mason jars without exception, hang the athletic socks up to dry, scrape the candlewax drippings off the floor. The visitor has the immense tenacity to pick the buckwheat seeds out of the cracks in the hardwood floor.

Meanwhile I direct the action from the sofa. The sofa, too, was left here by someone. Sometimes I wonder whether or not I too was simply forgotten here.

When I contract the corners of my mouth upwards, in fact, the visitor brings me a beer, whose cap he pops off before my eyes before retreating to the double doors backwards, like a real butler. He doesn't even trip and fall on the Persian carpet. I must say, I am delighted. It never crosses my mind to hire any other housecleaner or manservant, nor does it cross my mind to monetarily compensate the visitor for his activities. He is my very favorite (in the sense of: only) attendant. I almost never have to give an order twice. He washes the glasses until they sparkle, sucks the table completely free of crumbs with his mouth, shakes out the pillows like Old Mother Holle. The visitor is useful to me, not only because his stature enables him to reach the cobwebs in hard-to-reach places but also because I can bring him along to important functions (or so at least I imagine), leave him standing at the buffet, and point to him every now and then, whereupon he will wave back by wiggling his brushfingers with an idiotic smile on his face.

I suspect that the visitor is coloring every one of his eyelashes in its original color. He paints skin on his body so that it looks like skin. He makes little dots for freckles where he has freckles already. He washes his hairs so that later he can get them greasy again. Paints his lips with lip-colored lipstick. Every time the visitor's in the bathroom he spends hours in there just to look exactly the same afterwards as he did before.

When he heads for the sofa, he dangles his arms starting a good ten feet before he gets there, and then drops onto the cushions. He lies flat on the Freudian couch, cheek-lobes hanging to one side, arms seeming dead.

There are people who always seem to belong exactly where they happen to find themselves, even though they've only just then arrived there. There are people who never seem to not actually belong wherever they are, and/or seem to belong everywhere. I wonder if it's in the realm of the possible for someone to fuse with or melt into a sofa to the point where you can't tell whether that someone is visitor or sofa. I imagine it would be painful for the visitor if I now dropped onto the sofa myself. Aside from that, I wonder how long he intends to take a break and/or when he's going to get up and finally get back to peeling the parsnips.

Upon closer examination, incidentally, it is unclear whether the visitor's clothes are extremely vulgar. The crossing diagonal laces winding around his thighs, for instance, as if he were some kind of Cleopatra. I say to the visitor on the sofa: Those aren't pants, those are pajamas.

I am increasingly of the opinion that things go best for the visitor when he's being guided by a strong hand, that is to say, can grow to great heights along a firm structure. His growth is not my primary goal, per se, but whatever. What I'd actually like best would be for him to stay as small as he is now. For that to happen the visitor would have to be wrapped up tight in bandages, in the hope that this would retard his growth and thereby simplify the task of carrying his little body. Then I could bring him around the world in a suitcase someday, and if he looked particularly gruesome as a mummy I could show him at county fairs.

I attended a performance of the flea circus once. We all sat around a teeny-tiny circus ring, each member of the audience furnished with a magnifying glass. I remember that the grand finale was a race of flea-drawn mini-carriages, and that one of them suddenly stopped moving halfway along the track.

I likewise have a thing for shrunken heads, and frogs in glass bottles.

When it comes right down to it, though, I don't actually nurse the desire to travel the world with the visitor—only without him. But I won't leave the house to him without a fight. As long as there's a visitor to my sofa standing around my house I'm going to hold onto it. Besides, he brings the whole world here to me right at home, I don't even need to turn on the radio. The visitor feels like a ripple in the background. Sometimes I think: *Furniture Music*. He was simply there all of a sudden, as if he'd been there forever.

The visitor refuses to accept that the earth turns, that the sun alternatingly rises and sets. He takes every day like the first ever, gets out of his bed, puts on a blinded face, and waddles across the balcony, squinting at the surrounding panoramic vista—he knows no name for anything, has no memory at all of yesterday when I identified each individual mountain peak for him by means of a short lecture.

His morning rituals are a mystery to me. He twirls his hair with his fingers, slurps milky liquids from giant bowls, wears fake fur draped around his shoulders. The visitor is one big tackiness, an insult to the aesthetic eye. I feel sympathy for him, for he imitates a hippie or a woolly mammoth or some other extinct species, which doesn't much help him understand the present. He stays lost in his own thoughts while work is being done, while money is being shoveled into accounts, while the day is being given a certain rhythm. He, on the other hand, moves through time in circles. He refuses linearity. The minutes trickle uselessly past, down his furry arms, but he just keeps rocking in his rocking chair, his bloodshot eyes turned to look out the window.

There's no reason for the visitor to be aggressively mute. There's no reason for him to press his lips together and act like he's reading a book of high theory that rests on a foundation of discourse that's been superfluous for years. One cannot teach him anything; information just breezes right through him. In fact, I speak extra loud and enunciate extra clearly—like my father when he tries to speak French. I use my lips to draw the words in space. But the visitor just stares blankly, understanding nothing. I'd forget things too, if I could, but no, I'm a walking archive.

Something's not quite right about the visitor. That is to say, I know for certain that nothing is right about him. That nothing either suits him or matches the rest, that he's a collection of puzzle pieces from different puzzles, that his limbs are as though from different creatures in different epochs, sewn or glued together as it were, and he looks like a curiosity cabinet. Anyway, it's clear that the visitor's shape is very changeable—according to the growth of his beard, the time of day, whether the milk has spoiled, his whims, or whether the housework he is supposed to do has been carried out properly.

Still, today there is something that's not quite right about him above and beyond his steady-state not-quite-right-ness. He is staring into space, not touching the orange cake to his left, his face not brightening even when I (nonetheless) toss the business section of a newspaper in his general direction. The visitor is out of sorts. When I reluctantly kneel down next to him, he breaks out in a polyphonic howl, like an animal pipe organ in general and coupling cats in particular. With the best will in the world I find myself unable to translate these dissonances into meaningful propositions.

The visitor's nighttime howling would drive me up the wall if I still had a wall.

Don't get me wrong—it's not like I'm all that interested in the visitor. In no shape or form do I wonder what he's up to in his guest chamber, what fills his plastic bags to overflowing, why he spends hours on end screaming into the telephone. I'm not aggrieved in the least when he decides to go off somewhere and hide and refuses me his presence. His finally taking off his Cleopatra laces, or forgoing his hair-twirling, is incapable of disappointing me—if anything I rejoice, for what could be better than for the visitor's idiosyncrasies to take place behind closed doors where they're in no danger of driving me insane?

Now my phone's ringing too. It is advisable never to answer it, because you never know if it might be an unresolvable family conflict. You never know if it's my siblings, who call only when they want something I don't want to give them. You never know if it's my siblings calling to tell me that I need to take my crates and hit the road. My siblings have multiplied, had children, given expression to their own being in the world. Their reproductions in the form of children stand behind them like shadows and watch their backs. If my siblings used to be question marks, their children are exclamation points. My siblings, no longer moving through the world respectively alone but rather doubled and tripled, might be calling to say that their manifold existence now requires a many-roomed home, which, coincidentally, I as a single individual currently possess. They might be calling to inform me that while they are grateful that someone has periodically swept up the stones that have come loose from the facade, they now have sufficient hands at their disposal to do so, indeed more hands at their disposal than I have at mine.

Maybe I should answer the phone and tell my siblings that I, too, have multiplied and/or taken in a needy visitor who more than fills up the emptiness allegedly reigning in this house. Maybe I should tell them that it's just not right to kick a poor visitor out onto the street, one who cannot master our language (both the actual one and the cultural one) and who thus depends on my urgent help, i.e., shelter. Maybe I should tell them they're monsters who should be ashamed of themselves for proclaiming so openly the decadent and inappropriate desires brought about by their self-duplication via children!, I think, stretched out contentedly on the sofa.

When it gets light, the visitor slinks into my room to see if there might be any space next to my sleeping form, then lies down right outside the door, dozing like a cat, ears pricked up and turning this way and that toward every compass point in turn. When I come out of the room, in my grannie nightgown, he opens his eyes at once and laughs as though there were anything to laugh at. He has kept his shoes on while he slept.

It surpasses my understanding why the visitor is unable to keep the herd of vacuum cleaner nozzles in his room in check. Before the visitor's presence inaugurated the dawn of a new era, I entered that room countless times and always emerged fully unscathed. I admit that I did sometimes avail myself of a broom to keep the vacuum cleaner nozzles at bay and/or tame them by giving a nozzle a bonk on the muzzle. And of course I always made especially sure to have some lump of dirt or another ready for the vacuum cleaner nozzles, so as not to fall out of their good graces. I told my visitor from the beginning that he had to share the room with them, that I saw no possibility for resettling the vacuum cleaner nozzles, for in the end they seemed somehow particularly content there. On the complete contrary, I even have the feeling that the vacuum cleaner nozzle herd is doing better since the visitor laid his mattress among them. It may well be that the visitor is only putting forth the vacuum cleaner nozzles as an excuse for his messy, disheveled hair. The visitor lets his hairs grow unchecked instead of pomading them properly. I have tried to make it clear to him that there is a brush store in this small town, to which he might kindly pay a visit. I even offered to advance him the money for a hairbrush, so disturbing do I find his coiffure. Well, if the visitor is going to insist on ignoring my suggestions, he will have to be satisfied with the vacuum cleaner nozzle herd and/or its hairdressing expertise, which, with all due respect, seems to be not of the greatest. In general the vacuum cleaner nozzles prefer vacuuming on skin, where they leave behind dark patches. I have informed the visitor that this will be beneficial to his circulation and his health in general.

It's as if I wronged him in my dreams.

The visitor is standing in the doorway saying he wanted to take the blankets off someone in the middle of the night because that someone was sweating terribly, practically lying in a puddle, so he touched that someone and they gave an embarrassed laugh without waking up. In addition, he had tried to wake that someone up in the morning, jounced and joggled them, even pulled their hair slightly, and let the light into the room, yet they didn't move an inch, they just wrapped themself up in the blanket so tight it was impossible to unwind them, and then he had scratched at the blanket cocoon a little with his claws but unfortunately had to desist. Now he concludes his story, which is grammatically correct though in reality a total lie, and moves away from the doorway, which is in fact my doorway.

The visitor feels too comfortable here. The boots he wears, which aren't his, fit him perfectly. The fleece jacket I loaned him looks great on him. His body nestles into and up to things like they're made for him. He clings for dear life to some pompous book that his dirty fingertips leave marks on. Every now and then he spouts visions, which never come to pass. I never intended the visitor to conduct theoretical research on my behalf. It's time to pelt him with snowballs—big ones!

When night comes he falls silent, lies down on the bed, peers out from the down hood of his sleeping bag with his doelike eyes, and gives a grin by means of his sharp teeth. And then as he slowly pulls the zipper down and reveals an undershirt (and not much else!), and his white skin glistens forth in the candlelight, I know that it'd be better to lie down in the kitchen, where it is below freezing, than next to the naked visitor, whose potential progeny I have no intention of hatching.

Eventually I won't be able to remember the days anymore, only the nights, and/or the twilights, which will then collapse into one single recurring twilight. The visitor emits outlandish sounds in his sleep, accompanied by the chorus of snorting vacuum cleaner nozzles.

His chants penetrate through all the walls; I rock myself to the sound of the visitor's traumas. He has turned all the rooms into soporific saunas, turned up the heat throughout the house, even lit the fireplace. In any case, I absolutely must not fall asleep. Were I to succumb to sleep I would succumb to the visitor. He would drag me out of bed, haul me outside, lay me in the snow, deep-freeze me, and subsist on my meat and blood for weeks. I lie as if anesthetized, like ants in an anthill gently laid out after interloping trespassers exude their narcotic smoke.

In the morning, the visitor rises at the crack of dawn and signals good cheer, whereas I, completely shattered, can barely raise my head. I hear the visitor busy himself about the house and am worried. I furrow my brow, heave myself out of bed, and stomp off toward him. He is making a gigantic fire outside just to roast two sausages, a fire big enough to roast a cow, if not two cows, or a cow stuffed with a pig stuffed with a lamb stuffed with a chicken. I grind my teeth, say nothing, act nice, even generous, but the visitor's unnecessary fire, with him huffing and puffing into it like a crazy person, makes me doubt the rational nature of human beings in general and of this creature in particular. I grudgingly gnaw on my sausage, which the visitor has as it were pressed into my hand.

I feel like I've handed over the management of the household to an anarchist. The visitor is drunk and when he's drunk he looks like an eighties fashion model. He risks going blind from meandering through the blazing light of sun and snow without any eye protection, poking for the dunghill with a pitchfork. If the dunghill can't be found under the snow cover, it will be necessary to construct a new one, preferably in order to light it on fire. It is truly never wrong to contrive a blazing fire with fecal matter. I force the visitor to monitor the burning dunghill, with the words *We're not a hotel!,* and then I depart for the sun deck, where I page through a birding dictionary and sip fennel tea. Only occasionally does the wind carry over to me the smell, and the visitor's whimpering.

I cast shadows, sure, but not to stick the visitor into. Let him get a sunburn of his own.

Smoke rises out of the chimneys, and smoke comes out of our mouths puffing on rationed cigarettes: one per day. We are sitting, wrapped in fur, outside the snowed-in house, pressed against the facade, the dull sound of chopping wood in our ears, the white wine that cost three francs a bottle in our throats, and we are smoking our own flesh because we don't notice that the cigarettes clamped between our fingers have long since burned down. It's the last three seconds of the sun peeking over the mountaintop, the last three seconds when it's still day, not yet night.

The scenery is beautiful, but dull, is beautiful, but stupid.

I look through binoculars at the mountain peak across from us, where the military has put up tents and confiscated a couple of empty houses. Two soldiers are plowing swaths through the masses of snow. The visitor and I are doing everything as though for the last time, because we don't know how long the food will last, because we don't know how long the wood will last, because we don't know how long there'll be mountain air for us to breathe. The visitor and I share a piece of bread, and laugh, because we say: Nineteenth-century living!, but the laughter dies down quickly because we're not here to have fun, we're here to debate who'll go get more blankets, who more bread, who more bad white wine, who's meaner, who's funnier, who is just better, and I know that it's me and it'll always be me.

The drops of melting snow are putting on a rhythmical concert.

When at last the sound of a passing vehicle appears I run out to the road, in the hope that someone's coming, but the engine noise is just from two fighter jets on patrol. Like a dancing pair of lovers they execute a few formations, fly in parallel, part, return to each other, and eventually vanish behind the pyramid's point.

The pyramid lies there like an animal warming its back in the sun. Sometimes its shadow points straight at my house; moving slowly it impales my house, swallows it up entirely, and wraps it in black.

Yesterday I had no choice but to drink too much, and, swaying on my feet, I almost couldn't find my way home from the Roundel Bar; I waded blindly through the snow, suddenly ran across an ex-boyfriend and his current wife, and said hello with fake but apparently plausible friendliness, so that, after being taken aback at first, they both started to even be happy to see me. I can therefore say in good conscience that my presence is, generally speaking, extremely sought-after and desired. Even when, for instance, one of the countless spiders in my house decides to die, it prefers to do so in or next to my bed.

Even as a child I knew I was needed. In a restaurant I would play with a stuffed giraffe in the play corner; when we had to leave, my parents said that the giraffe wasn't mine so I had to leave it there, but I could pet it one more time as a goodbye. At that I clasped the giraffe's neck in my little hands and screamed over and over: But the giraffe needs me, it needs me! They had to peel my fingers, which were really very tiny at the time, off the giraffe's neck one by one while my tantrum continued.

Yesterday, as I said, certain things alcoholically slipped out of my grasp as I sat at the bar of the Roundel and the waiter, who was behaving just awfully, urged me with a diabolical grin to keep tossing down double tequilas, with lemon, but no salt. He had shaved with ludicrous precision; his body trembled with boredom. He presently tried to discern my sexual orientation, interpreting my un-made-up face as lesbian and subsequently pressing into my hand the business card of a writer who had made it his task to preach the existence of extraterrestrial life. In general I am increasingly disgusted by the exoticization of things, and accordingly I wear wool pants with my sports sweater tucked in; in other ways too I dislike having anyone tell me what I can and can't do. My mother, in fact, one day found it necessary to come and apologetically explain to my kindergarten teacher in person that my clothes were chosen entirely by me.

Interestingly enough, the purchase of a red jacket changed my everyday life for the better. The color possessed such force and blatant pushiness that, quite naturally, every eye turned away from it and seemed altogether unable to see me. At this very moment I've gotten so warm that I'd really like to take the red jacket off, but I'm afraid of my presence that would emerge from beneath it.

The visitor has it good since he's barely ever noticed anyway. I've told him so, many a time, but his spirits remain dark and heavy as lead. He goes jogging through the woods in oversized leather gloves and a neon-pink down vest. He can barely lift his legs, his back is humped, the corners of his mouth droop wet-earthwards. As a result, I have consciously and rationally decided to avoid the visitor and his despair.

It is a widespread custom on the paternal side of my family to make oneself understood with the pronoun "one." The distancing quality of "one" is especially close to my heart. My father and Uncle Walter used to drive out to Alsace and sit hunched over their fish prix fixes. I was quite young when I started going with them, petting Uncle Walter's boisterous German Shepherd on the head, who when she died of old age was replaced by an even more boisterous one, and so forth, until at some point the dog was completely wild, while my Uncle Walter, though spry and robust, did inescapably keep getting older and thus smaller and dragged along by the dog's leash. As a listener I was always fascinated by the fact that they were erecting a mysterious—in the sense of: nonexistent—buffer around their personal opinions by saying "one." I understood from that point on that my own story did not exist on its own: my uncle's story was unavoidably bound up with it, as well as with the stories of all the other customers in the Alsatian fish restaurant and beyond.

The visitor's story, which isn't mine and which nonetheless is increasingly becoming mine, weighs heavily upon me. The only thing is, just because I can bear a heavy load doesn't mean I want to—not by a long shot.

The slightest breeze is enough to open the front door of the house, but the truth is I sometimes wish I didn't have a front door at all. Even before, people used to go in and out of my house as they pleased, especially in. They would sit on the sofa or next to my bed and I seemed to recognize them, or sometimes seemed not to. I have never yet encountered someone who didn't either read my notes, put on my black fur jacket, or secretly try to sleep in my bed. Again and again I've had to sit down with these aforementioned people and have a little talk with them. At the same time, I find it absolutely ghastly to have to constantly listen to people. I try to forbid the visitor, too, from talking, especially as long as he doesn't have anything interesting to say. What he says flows right past me, running as I picture it straight into the drain, which is soon going to be completely clogged up with his hairs. The visitor has the problem of not mastering the language, for instance he gets idioms mixed up or uses the wrong word endings, to the point where I get tired of having to figure out what he means. I have let the visitor talk a lot, at great length, although in a language I don't know. I believe I may in good conscience disavow the responsibility for the visitor that one might ascribe to me. He already said he was prepared to serve me, and so I'm in no way responsible for him. I only wish I had no jurisdiction over more of the world.

One time, this happened: I got into a tram and stood next to a seemingly ownerless bicycle. When the tram started moving, the bike did too and in fact seemed to be of a mind to fall over. Now, it would have been possible for me—as the only person standing nearby—to catch the bike, which, however, never crossed my mind, since it wasn't my conveyance, and so not my responsibility, and so, without batting an eye, I let it crash to the floor and then nimbly breezed off, swishing my wool dress around my calves.

It's no mystery to me when buses crash into walls either. I've recently noticed again how bus drivers have to wait at every station with freakish patience until all the people—elderly, geriatric, indigent—betake themselves onto or off of the bus with infinite slowness, until they sit down, or at least hold on, and he can at last close the door—in slow motion—at which point one more person lumbers over to the bus after all and the whole procedure starts again from the top. I feel sick to my stomach just thinking about that bus dragging itself at a crawl from station to station only to repeat the same snailish ceremony at each one. Yes, it is almost incomprehensible to me that there are people who day after day can actually endure such proceedings, or even be perfectly happy to perform them.

I've never said I'm proud of how wicked I am. And yet I must admit I've come to terms with it relatively quickly. I find that I have basically always had great trouble telling people what they wanted to hear from me. I have always suffered under a strange relationship to the spoken word. As a result I've driven various people crazy by keeping quiet for too long a period of time or seeming entirely lost in my own thoughts while muttering an endless monologue they didn't dare interrupt.

The visitor glances up as if looking for supertitles. He won't find the answer there. There are no supertitles. I mean what I say. What I say needs no translation and cannot be translated by anyone. The visitor sits back down in the rocking chair and continues paging through a dictionary with the goal of better mastering the language.

Sometimes, when I look at this visitor who just won't obey properly and so stoops out of spite, I remember back to my own stooped dynasty. My grandfather, my uncle Walter, my father, the whole series of hunchbacks who, under the stern gaze of the fathers, grandfathers, and great-grandfathers who preached in their sect tried to make themselves seem as small as possible. And now that they've all died or gone away, there's really only me left to uphold this tradition of stooped existence. But rather than let my shoulders droop, as my family tree would have it, I feel a great desire to puff myself up.

When the visitor opens his mouth to say something, I love beating him to the punch.

Today I am going to start drawing up a set of rules and regulations that will encompass, if possible, every point the visitor is expected to comply with. It'll be of service to everybody. The set of rules can be extended at will. I imagine it as a kind of Holy Scripture that the visitor can keep next to his bed. If and when he has questions—for I believe he has many—he can look up the answers to them in the rulebook instead of bothering me while I'm working. Unlike the Bible, it will not be a collective scripture but one composed by me alone. I'm sick and tired of composing collective scriptures. Admittedly I have never taken part in composing a collective scripture, but I imagine it would be tedious for me if anyone else tried to contribute his or her opinion. It's important to me that the visitor understand that going around in his underwear here is by no means appropriate.

Incidentally, there was a lot of work I should have been doing, but I'm prepared to let everything be and/or drop for the sake of this visitor and instruct him instead. In fact, I buy him a decent pair of pants in the supermarket. Then I buy him a pair of slippers, a couple of books, I think I might even cut his toenails while he's asleep, the way my parents used to do for me when I had yet again refused to cut my nails and was walking around with claws.

Eventually more people were standing in front of my house wanting a room here as well. Eventually there was a downright line of people leading away from my door, perfectly prepared to stab each other with their umbrellas if doing so would result in a place in my house. These people wear gold-rimmed glasses to imitate the visitor. They tie paintbrushes to their fingers or pull zipperless rain ponchos over their heads. One even carries an aquarium with deep black fish bustling around in it. Are those my siblings, complete with their shadows, taking their places in that line? In my house there is only one room I am generous enough to rent out, I cry, and I slam the door shut.

Nevertheless, whenever I'm in the mood, I insinuate to the visitor that he would be easy to replace. Sometimes I even wink at this or that hopeful tenant through the kitchen window. Then I imagine that if I took in a second visitor, his feet would have a different shape and as a result would make my Birkenstocks take on a different shape. I could keep the old visitor's paraphernalia for the new visitor, tailored or shortened if need be, or for instance cross out the embroidered letters on the cotton table napkins and embroider a new name next to the crossed-out old one.

I am told that my siblings came and rang the doorbell, asking about me and inquiring into my health. After waiting in line for hours and finally reaching the front, they were apparently astounded to discover a guest in the house, but were delighted, they said, to make his acquaintance. They asked a few more questions, to be polite—Who are you? Where are you from? Are those brushfinger hairs real?—and then asked the visitor to call me, which he did at once, although without success, so there was nothing left for them to do but ask him to pass along the message that they would like to see me in person again or at least be able to reach me by phone.

I don't know who was lying more: the visitor or my siblings.

I tell the visitor that should he ever again have the misfortune to talk to my siblings or anyone else, he can inform them that I am very sorry to have missed them, and that I'll get in touch with them as soon as I can find the time, but that this rarely happens. The thing about me is I am a very busy person, so to speak drowning in work, after all I am working on a Holy Scripture, notes for which are lying around everywhere, to the point where I can sometimes barely dig myself out, plus I have this very houseguest to worry about, who has to be supervised and managed, yes, actually he needs my help with almost everything he gets it into his head to do, he's so not independent, he can't even dust to my satisfaction, and he definitely has a strange relationship to the vacuum cleaner nozzles, but that's a story for another time. The important thing, I say, is this: He should absolutely inform whomever he's talking to that he, the visitor, may seem small but is going to get bigger and bigger to the point where all ten rooms will be needed in order to house him, and thus it is indeed impossible for them—that is, my dear siblings—to move into the house, in case this should be the reason for their turning up, although I certainly appreciate the urgency of their wanting to, after all they have shadows underpinning and reinforcing this urgency, or to put it another, better way, children, but living in this house is precisely as urgent for the visitor, if not indeed somewhat more. He showed up scratching at my door, dressed in rags, without the slightest zest for life, so I took pity on him and granted him temporary asylum until he would be able to turn his rags back into respectable items of clothing and/or find a little joie de vivre somewhere or other, which, alas, has not yet turned out to be the case. The visitor is even now—as has certainly not escaped their notice—a downright pitiful figure, so I would implore them to muster up all their humanity and let the visitor as well as my humble self remain in the house a little bit longer, we both would be immensely grateful.

Whenever I open the cupboard where I store my food—valuable food-stuffs, since they have by now become more or less rarities—all the items I find have been nibbled on. And just because I've let the visitor keep his slices of rye bread in my cupboard, that in no way means he is authorized to go in and out of the cupboard however he pleases! There are house rules, specifically and elaborately formulated, printed, and laminated!

One time, incidentally, I laminated a beetle alive. And ever since the visitor's moved in, absolutely everything has been attacked by moths.

Never again will I invite anyone over. Never again will I prepare an aperitif with delectable regional dishes. The visitor's a drinker either way. The good white wine is gone in a flash, the cheesy nibbles—despite his claim of lactose intolerance—gobbled down in a flash. My own tolerance is turning not merely to intolerance but to full-on irreconcilability. The visitor is impossible, and the only way I can think of to oppose his grinning at my peculiar dialectal inventions is by turning up the popular folk music, which to my ear too is torture but which, first of all, is part of our cultural identity and, second of all, makes the visitor drop his glass of white wine in horror, which (thanks to wise foresight) is not in fact glass, but plastic.

I would advise anyone who wants to get rid of a visitor forthwith to starve him out. The containers of edibles in the cupboards have to be vacuum-sealed and welded shut. Grocery shopping must cease immediately. The pantry is to be locked with a varied and copious assortment of locks. The visitor, as soon as he feels himself to be alone, will march hungrily over to the cupboards, but he must not find anything to eat. This will make his spirits turn foul, with immediate effect. Yet he will not under any circumstances let it show, for he must claim to be grateful—must be full to bursting with gratitude, through and through, a sentiment nourished by the temporary roof over his head, that is: his tolerated stay. The hungry visitor, after this initial bout of bad temper, will fall into a lethargy that will make him submissive. He will sit at the table and look at me from haggard eye sockets. Whatever I command him to do, he will accept with an absent nod. He will say, seeming in the process completely insane: I'm eating increasingly healthily and getting increasingly sick. It's time to start drinking again. Am I a fish stranded on shore? Only when someone douses me in liquid do I come back to life.

Then the visitor will break out in laughter.

During the night, once the visitor falls into his nightmarish sleep, I will measure the width of his bite.

Due to sleep disturbances caused by the visitor, I've started staying up all night watching rebroadcasts of the final rounds of snooker tournaments, and I find myself increasingly delighted by the placidity with which the players move around the table. Only their glances speed this way and that, aimed at the various balls gracefully awaiting the blow that will transport them directly into one of the pockets. Then the trembling, the faltering, the spinning, when a ball refuses to vanish into the darkness. Some snooker players smile when one of their shots fails to come off, for example Mark the Shark, who possesses in general the appearance, and especially the whitened smile, of a Hollywood star. But usually the balls obey their destiny and travel straight into the hole as if on rails.

If someone is "snookered," they're caught in a trap. "Snookering" the other player is sometimes a player's last chance at victory, or, when not, it hastens the opponent's downfall. The "snookered" player has to speed in the form of a ball across the green surface via every imaginable detour. Anyone who gets free of the trap in this fashion is loudly and generously applauded by the audience, otherwise the spectators almost always stay silent. Whoever's turn it isn't has to sit next to the green table, sipping a drink. He can do no more than, at most, demonstratively turn his head aside and gaze off at the actual spectators to avoid looking on at his possible downfall—thereby running the risk of losing the narrative on the table and control of the game altogether.

I have only one pair of eyes that I can direct at people.

The visitor, meanwhile, lies on the Persian carpet and doesn't let anyone move him off it. He looks sickly, summons me over, has me cover him with a blanket, and falls at once into a comatose sleep. He snores away like a stupid rock, now and then startles up out of his nightmares, then turns back to stone. Since at the moment I'd rather be watching Mark the Shark nonchalantly swinging the bridge stick through the air, I wrap the visitor up in the Persian carpet without further ado so that I can drag him qua sleeping carpet-roll out of the living room. *Drag* has always been one of my favorite verbs, incidentally.

I drag the visitor complete with his carpet around my house, intentionally bumping him into all the corners and doorframes. Then I let him, complete with his carpet, tumble down the stairs, but he doesn't even consider waking up. So then I drag him farther, into the guest chamber, which cannot be called mine ever since the visitor annexed it. The vacuum cleaner nozzles part knowingly as I enter the room. One wants to be a nice person, after all, one wants to help the visitor, his snoring might well be the expression of serious war trauma, a consequence of great loneliness, a likeness of nomadic existence. The visitor is as empty as the bottle of gin I had no choice but to drink in its entirety the day before yesterday, in despair at his never-ending visit.

And still the visiting roll sleeps, cool and cylindrical as a cucumber, and I wouldn't begrudge him this if only it didn't disturb my own sleep so much. The time has really come at last when I need to lie down in a bed and shut my eyes. There is no longer any question of sleep in my case, needless to say. It's merely a matter of tossing and turning, wrapping myself in and unwrapping myself out of the blankets, standing up and lying down in turn, a circular process.

From time to time I run a lint roller over the visitor's sleeping face. As I do so my hair lies almost heavily on my shoulders, like a carpet, even though it has always weighed quite little.

My back is completely stiff. I lie pharaonically in bed and try to pick up the books next to the bedframe but my fingertips can only just touch the books' spines. I am a mummy, forced to rely on the visitor. I ring for him and he appears in the doorway at once, actually it's exactly like he's been waiting there all along. He gives me a pitying look, despite there being no reason at all to do so. I am an imposing person—even if one with a weak spine. I don't like it when people criticize me for my curved posture, much less when they try to stretch me out.

Whenever anyone asked me a question at school, too, I was guaranteed not to know the answer even though I'd known it before, i.e., pre-questioning. Never once in a single classroom have I spoken voluntarily, and I have been constantly reprimanded for that. Since then it's really been impossible for me to raise my hand, and anyway I had better things to do, for instance flinging tennis balls around the schoolyard.

Now I fling nothing, now I can't even raise my head, despite it being, in general terms, quite small and light. The visitor says that it's winter making me so stiff. He too suffers from the cold that comes creeping through the cracks in the windows, he says. He is not especially well armed or equipped against this cold, he goes on, so he must admit that sometimes at night he throws my red jacket over him, it's very pleasant, and the vacuum cleaner nozzles cuddle up under his blanket too, sometimes.

Now he wants to feed me sweet potatoes and peanut butter. He bakes fruitcake whose slices are like the cross-section of a human body. I press my lips together. I don't want to eat any human cross-section. I'd rather starve than let the visitor poison me. Meanwhile the visitor sits next to my bed, even though I keep pointing him toward the door. He smiles politely when I eventually, millimeter by millimeter, slide down along the wall of the room.

Since the visitor's arrival, the lemons have lost all their taste.

Since the visitor's arrival, the sun has set not long after it's risen.

Since the visitor's arrival, one finds oneself old and sick, and all kinds of dirt is stuck to one's winter coat; one does intend to remove it with a lint roll, but then one finds oneself facing a hopeless task.

Since the visitor's arrival, people have been in a bad mood, the houses small, and the windows drafty. You press all your extremities against the radiators and sip tea while paper-thin slices of peeled lemon float around the teacup like jellyfish.

Since the visitor's arrival, a vitamin deficiency has broken out. One feels so tired that one's arms hang down, to the left and right of one's body, and swing back and forth; one is unable to lift one's hand, for example in greeting, is unable to set one foot in front of the other, that is: walk, so one stands around like a telephone pole. One nevertheless drags oneself to the doctor and accepts all kinds of prescriptions for medicaments to expel the gravitational pull from one's limbs. One nevertheless drags oneself to the pharmacy and runs through the alphabet stem to stern, swallows the alphabet soup down in the form of pills, tablets, and capsules, tosses them down one's throat, and yet one knows: the problem will go away only when the visitor does.

If the visitor truly is an illness, there is no cure. I am inconsolable, because the illness by the name of *visitor* will crush me. I moan, I howl, it'll kill me in the end. I see expensive treatments and surgeries in my future, far surpassing my bank account's ability to deal with them.

I'm tempted to burst into a fit of whooping cough.

I never cried in front of other children. Not even when I jumped into an empty well headfirst. Also not when my childhood boyfriend, let's call him Laurenz, played a sex scene for me on the TV in my mother's bedroom, fast-forwarding the VHS tape right to the spot where a naked man and a naked woman appeared, sitting in bed, wedged together. Laurenz was showing me this, he said, because the idea had spontaneously come over him to reconstruct this scene or something along its lines with me. I was not completely opposed.

Up in the attic a few days later we went looking for an appropriate place and lay down in a dusty corner on top of each other (although clothed) as a test run. But instead of getting back up off the floor and brushing the dust off, Laurenz suddenly held me tight, squeezing the air out of me. I waved my arms around but couldn't push him off me. He didn't let go. He stared at me through his glasses, and when, after a few minutes, he finally released me, he acted like it had been just a joke, which I should now laugh about—so I laughed.

One time, I invited the neighbor girl to hide in my closet and peep out through the crack of the door when Laurenz and I were kissing. Laurenz didn't know about that, nor did he know that I was playing actually good childhood sex-games with the neighbor girl.

It's cramped in a bathtub. Especially when two people are lying in there. The only real possibilities are for one person to lie in and/or on the other, or for both to sit with their legs tucked in like little parcels. If they go for the parcel option, the parts of their bodies that are out of the water will quickly get chilly, if not indeed catch cold, looming up above the surface like pointy icebergs. It is therefore necessary to coat oneself qua parcel in hot water, placing each side of the body in the water for one to two minutes. In so doing, it is important to make sure that one nostril remains located above water at all times. The gargling underwater nostril, meanwhile, contributes to one's auditory well-being.

These techniques can also be applied to lying on a sofa. If everyone involved leans their back against an armrest and places their legs on the sofa, they can meet in the middle of the sofa. Depending on the length or shortness of the piece of furniture in question, partial overlapping might occur. Should the overlapping of legs be in fact desired, said legs can be stacked above and below one another at will. Feet can be placed between the other person's legs or on their belly. Place one Scottish wool blanket on top of this leg salad. The only thing is, sometimes a bare leg will slip out from under this blanket, toward the floor, but usually it will quickly be pulled back in.

When the decision is made to lie on a sofa in a state of not merely overlapping but full-on covering, one hopes that the piece of furniture in question has at its disposal a sufficient total length in relation to the supine body length.

The visitor's spine rasps against mine.

When he lies down on the sofa, I lie down on the Persian carpet. When he comes to join me on the Persian carpet, I vault onto the sofa. I suspect it is inherent in the visitor's and my respective natures that we never end up encamping in the same place, only and precisely somewhere the other one isn't. Really I don't know what the deal is with this sofa. I cannot deny that I brought it into the house myself, even though I don't like sitting down somewhere and never have, but now this sofa just stands around, even though I have never intended to use it. It simulates living, residing, home, one might even say homeland, while in reality it just gets in the way and spoils any good mood I might otherwise be in.

Moreover, the visitor lies around on it constantly, as though that's what it was made for.

Sofas are ugly, even assuming you're prepared to blow all your savings on one. Sofas are uncomfortable, especially when one has a visitor trying to rub his lovely feet against mine. Sofas turn travelers into sedentaries, extraverts into introverts, protesters into sleepers. Anyone who has a sofa has decided to settle down, that is: capitulate. Basically, to die soon. But I'm not ready to die! Not for the sofa, not for the visitor. Tomorrow I will order the visitor to get up from the sofa and carry it out onto the street to be taken away. I'm sure there are plenty of people with suicidal tendencies who'd love to have it.

I laugh and snort whenever I see the visitor—his limbs are much too long. The visitor's limbs flop around and have no function whatsoever. I laugh and snort, coffee comes spurting out my nose, when I see the visitor's head, whose narrowness can be explained only with recourse to a tragic genetic accident. The visitor then withdraws, with an expression of ridiculous confidence on his face, although in fact he is the most pitiful creature ever to swagger across this hardwood floor.

Or, as someone once remarked when I once again made a face that caused her to burst out laughing and send me out of the classroom to stand in the hall—I'm afraid I might have even been in high school at the time: How is it even possible to look so horrid?

It must be some years back now that a young man once had the nerve to tell me I look a lot better from the front than in profile. Another young man—this must have been even longer ago—did once praise my legs in the highest possible terms, but then told me about a friend to whom he'd showed a photo of me and who, upon observing my likeness, had said he couldn't quite decide whether he would describe me as attractive. I slept with both of them anyway.

The visitor rubs his shoulder against mine, which makes me immediately fly into a rage. Am I cat furniture? Am I a salt lick? The visitor thinks too highly of himself, he wants to make out with me. It makes me laugh. What could be further from my mind than the idea of kissing our little troublemaker?

I think I've finally found a painting in which I can recognize myself. It's of a lion, under a blazing sun that colors the sky blood-red, digging its teeth into an antelope's back, while the prey peers up at its murderer with a mixture of fear and desire. The onlookers—two birds, one leopard—traipse through the treetops and ferns practically fainting with lust, the way people imagined ferns in the early twentieth century.

I have rarely taken any special enjoyment in bodily contact with other people. One time, collecting chestnuts in the park, an older gentleman spoke to me—I must have been about eight—and I didn't have any better response than to drop the chestnuts and run off into the distance.

In judo class, too, I had the bad luck to find myself lying in a *kata gatame* hold under a boy bigger and heavier than me. He had long hair, which hung down wet and sweaty in my face, and what I needed to do was fling him off me, lightning fast, toss him over my head in fact, but I couldn't do it—my mother said: I couldn't do it *yet*—and in truth I barely made it to an orange belt, and shortly before achieving my orange belt I said no thanks, I don't need this orange, and the rainbow colors to follow, I don't need them either, and so I took off the white robe, which looks like a bathrobe actually, folded it up, placed it on the floor, and quit judo class.

Suddenly I seem to have some kind of stench sticking to me, and I can't quite figure it out. It's like with my dreams at night. They are all either about living in a house or about ratlike mythical creatures that stare anthropomorphically at me, lie down on my chest, and put their thick black claws on my throat.

The visitor and I act out fairy tales. Today it's "The Wolf and the Seven Kids." My black fleece jacket is supposed to imitate the wolf's fur. I speak in a high voice as if I've eaten chalk; I stick my paws disguised white with chalk through the doorway. The visitor, playing all seven of the young goats, opens the door for me, and I pounce on him at once. I yank him out from under the sofa, from behind the wardrobe, from behind the curtain; I find him under the carpet, under the blanket on the bed. I gobble up all six visitors head to toe, grinding my teeth into their soft flesh. Only, I can't find the seventh.

Afterwards, the visitor imagines he's being particularly original in suggesting that we switch characteristics. He wants to play a gobbling goat while I play a defenseless wolf. The visitor's belly sticks out from under his shirt, he's so full, having eaten me up.

We could found the worst moving company of all time. We would always show up too late, would always be in a bad mood, would bump the most valuable piano into everything; the corners of every piece of furniture would be blunted or broken off, the stairway walls scratched. While hauling the pieces that are much too heavy for us, we'd scream constantly. We wouldn't carry anything, actually, just scrape it along the floor, or else throw it right out the window. We would then sweep up the shattered furniture lying on the street and toss the pieces and smithereens into a van.

Today, in fact, we thought about what it would be like to empty out my house and put completely new furniture into the resulting void, for instance Swedish design from the '60s. We're almost pretending to be a couple, maybe engaged, or married. We're almost pretending to be two lovers lying naked in bed discovering that their bodies fit each other's like a glove, neither knowing anything about the other and yet knowing everything about the other.

Luckily I'm not crazy enough to believe in love.

My family consists of respectable people who are similar in that they face life from a slight distance—exactly as though they found it a little embarrassing to have a life at all. Contact with my family is wonderful because none of them ever tries to get closer to me in any exaggerated way. For example, the people who number among my family do not call me often—except for my siblings—just as I too phone them extremely rarely. No one likes to ask for help in my family; they prefer to carry the most abominable burden around on their own until their shoulders break.

Both my parents and my siblings were furnished with intermittent back problems and therefore had to get numerous massages. It turned out that the easiest thing to do was hire a family masseuse, on call for any of them as soon as any problem loomed on any of their horizons. The masseuse was on close terms with the spinal columns that flop around in all our backs, unable to decide to settle down into one fixed location. It's hard to take on a burden with bones that drift off. I wonder what it is that makes our family's spinal columns so restless. Someone who married into the family even had to have two broken vertebrae reassembled and fixed in place with screws.

Aside from that, I remember my parents' polite looks when I was a child showing them something. I could always see from those looks that they, my parents, were just waiting for me, the youngest, to grow up so they could go away. I can't hold it against them—I feel exactly the same way vis-à-vis the visitor. My parents always started from the false assumption that I was there simply because that was how it was supposed to be; all my life I've felt a great desire to break with this self-evidence, yet I never have. My parents beat me to it and started a new life somewhere else, far away. They did exactly what always stood clearly written in their eyes and that I therefore also wanted to do, but I never could. I wanted to abandon my parents, but my parents abandoned me. I would go visit them if only there wasn't a visitor residing in the house. I made a commitment to this visitor and so I can't just drop everything and leave. His fur needs brushing daily.

Don't brag, my mother would have said. I think I got it from her: my tendency to delight in tiny objects and creatures.

I feel so stormy sometimes, and whenever we drift apart the visitor holds onto me across the ravine between our beds. The veins in his hands like mountain streams, his light-brown eyes framed by lashes, his hair like a halo around his head.

I have control over him, but no longer have any idea how to exert it against him.

Sometimes I worry that he's chafing me raw with his solicitude. I try to assign him the most impossible tasks, but he brilliantly masters them all. He used to be a howling wolf one wanted to muzzle before one's eardrums shattered, and now he won't stop going around with the friendliest smile, practically a grin, on his face. He takes delight in woodworms, in tractors driving by, in balloons going up. Just like that the visitor has become a blithe spirit, happy to spend hours busy doing the most boring things, which he can then cross off his list with a bright shining highlighter—and bright shining eyes. The visitor exudes peace and relaxation; every day he rejects anew this world that's falling apart. He uses the sharpest axes, saws, and knives and is never in danger of hurting himself. The visitor's new optimism vis-à-vis life is like a screeching power saw in my ears. His intact moral state like a thorn in my eye. The visitor is exemplary, but I don't need any exemplars, I need a cleaning man or lady for my house and home, especially my house, since I don't exactly have a home.

The visitor also tries to capture the pink sunsets and mountain panorama with his cellphone camera.

While he goes around filling all and sundry with joy, the deepest imaginable abysses sprout up inside me. I never intended for the visitor, a lost soul I took in out of the goodness of my heart, to slip out of his sadness. I say *Sit!*, but the visitor acts like he doesn't hear me. His original owner clearly neglected to enroll him in and graduate him from dog obedience school. If the visitor ever stops satisfying me with his brushfingers, things might get uncomfortable.

Since the visitor's arrival, I've been clenching my teeth so hard that they not only grind but threaten to crack apart—according to what a dentist told me yesterday.

Since the visitor's arrival, I've fallen into a dentist's clutches. He wants to extract all these teeth, for no reason, and charge horrific sums, and he advertises these services on his website with psalms.

Since the visitor's arrival, I've wished that I understood basically anything about psalms, or churches, or religious leaders.

Since the visitor's arrival, I've constantly forgotten who I was, who I am, and where I belong.

Since the visitor's arrival, the wine has remained wine.

Since the visitor's arrival, this very same wine has gone to my head, and stained my teeth blue and red—the dentist is appalled.

Since the visitor's arrival, every loaf of carrot cake I've tried to bake has turned out black, and every loaf of black bread has turned out yellow.

Since the visitor's arrival, I've started baking, but I'm going to stop again, because when it comes right down to it I'm not a housewife and have no intention of becoming one, even if I do own and/or rent a house.

Since the visitor's arrival, the house has been doing very badly.

Since the visitor's arrival, the facade has been crumbling and in fact the entire property has been shrinking.

Since the visitor's arrival, I've been losing rooms in the house like earrings; I look for them everywhere yet I can never find them.

Since the visitor's arrival, the whole house has shrunk down to a single tiny room.

In general, many things have shrunk since the visitor's arrival, including my bank balance and the tomatoes in the fridge that no one eats.

Since the visitor's arrival, there have been constant blood-red full moons or new moons or other bad omens.

Since the visitor's arrival, the constellations have shifted and so I have considered requesting a horoscopic consultation, even though I always used to insist on never believing in astrology.

Since the visitor's arrival, the plants have been growing tall and bearing fruit on all the balconies except mine, even the plants that normally don't bear fruit.

Since the visitor's arrival, I've walked the streets muttering evilly.

Since the visitor's arrival, people on the street have been staring strangely at me.

Since the visitor's arrival, I've had no more friends, no happiness.

Since the visitor's arrival, someone has been playing the recorder constantly outside my house, despite having never taken a single recorder lesson.

Since the visitor's arrival, I myself have deeply yearned to go door to door playing the recorder, despite having never taken a single recorder lesson.

Since the visitor's arrival, I've been working on a song that I call

"You Have to Leave Now," even though I can neither sing nor play any instrument, except the recorder.

Since the visitor's arrival, I've called my mother long-distance and baselessly accused her of all sorts of things, to which she responds by crying and pressing the hangup button.

Since the visitor's arrival, I've been evil and hunchbacked; I don't want to get up in the morning; my head feels so heavy on the pillow that I can barely lift it anymore.

Since the visitor's arrival, I've found that heads in general are quite heavy.

Since the visitor's arrival, I've wondered why we even have heads when they're so often turned in the wrong direction.

Since the visitor's arrival, I've wanted nothing whatsoever to do with any heads, and especially not with the visitor's beautiful one.

Since the visitor's arrival, I've enjoyed holding that head between my hands.

Since the visitor's arrival, I've had no desire to read anymore, not even the damn newspaper.

Since the visitor's arrival, I've lost all faith in fate.

Since the visitor's arrival, not one funny pun has occurred to me.

Since the visitor's arrival, everyone has been able to do everything better than me.

Since the visitor's arrival, I've wondered why he never lets me win when we play cards, even though I'm playing cards only because he wants to. I hate games.

Since the visitor's arrival, I've wanted all the more urgently to get away from here, but he holds me back, because his head is made of stone and I'm not Obelix from *Asterix and Obelix.*

Since the visitor's arrival, I've grown stupider and stupider. I read but I don't understand anything.

Since the visitor's arrival, history has been transformed, truths have shifted, a completely new perspective on the world has become necessary.

Since the visitor's arrival, slaves have risen up from the grave and noble masters laid down in those graves instead.

Since the visitor's arrival, the negative has turned positive and vice versa.

Since the visitor's arrival, new forms of government have had to be invented.

Since the visitor's arrival, I have cried no more tears—instead the tears cry me.

Since the visitor's arrival, I haven't been able to leave the house, all I do is wait for him to come home.

Since the visitor's arrival, the hawks have fallen from the sky.

Since the visitor's arrival, . . .

Since the visitor's arrival, . . .

Since the visitor's arrival, . . .

Since the visitor's arrival, . . .

Since the visitor's arrival, my jokes have gotten stuck in my throat, and not even the dentist with his forceps has been able to extract them.

Since the visitor's arrival, I've had no love left to give to anyone—except him.

Since the visitor's arrival, the house has been clean, but I never wanted to eke out a sterile existence in the first place.

Since the visitor's arrival, two adorable rainbows have arched above this too-clean house.

Since the visitor's arrival, I've seen everything blurrily, even though I used to have the eyes of a hawk.

Since the visitor's arrival, people have been dropping dead all around me.

Since the visitor's arrival, I've wondered why nobody gets worked up over the fact that we all must die.

Since the visitor's arrival, I've gotten lost in a head full of thoughts and woken up hours later in a different place.

Since the visitor's arrival, the light has glared into the pupils of my eyes from the side, blinding me.

The fish are dead, but that was already obvious. They're floating on their backs on the surface of the aquarium's water, but that was already obvious. They met a miserable end, one after the other. One fish per day. The ones still living looked sadly up at their lifeless fellow swimmers—knowing full well that they would be next. I carefully scoop the dead fish out of the water in a cupped hand, their teeny-tiny scales glittering up at me. I wrap their almost weightless bodies in napkins and cotton wool, make little monuments to them out of matchsticks, and bury them outside the house as the weak winter sun sets in the fog.

A suspicion popped into my head and I can't get free of it: the visitor sucked all the oxygen out of the fish.

As I pick up the tombs and stick them in the snow cover—although, by virtue of a fish's scanty bodily volume, there is hardly anything to bury—he stays sitting at the kitchen table, which I never actually gave him permission to use, trying to pick up tangerine slices with his fur-covered brushfingers.

Woe is me, how I blame myself, I could slap myself. When the visitor wandered by, when he stood on the doormat with his ridiculous plastic bags and his shabby clothes, I knew I could have ignored the doorbell, burrowed under the blankets, slammed the shutters closed, never opened the door again, I think, resting on the shovel, which is just a little toy shovel. My gravediggerly reflection gazes back at me from the kitchen window, superimposed on the form of the visitor in the kitchen, who as a result has four eyes and is now peering out at me with all four of them.

Later I see the visitor standing at the fish graves. He even appears affected, moved, by their deaths. When I look closer at him, I see the fish scales still glittering between his teeth. I never much liked these fish and/or never took much trouble about them—someone who used to live with me, and subsequently didn't, left them here. Perhaps the visitor's arrival made me forget the fish even more than I had already forgotten them anyway. People say fish are easy to take care of, at least I always acted on that assumption.

The visitor holds out a little plant to me, a furred cactus, as a condolence, but I'm sobbing so hard that I can barely take it from him.

Laurenz liked to lie to me too. He claimed to own a little dinosaur that he kept in a cage in his room, but whenever I went over to his house to see the creature at last, Laurenz said that his father was just then out walking it. Even though I knew full well: Laurenz didn't have a father.

I never saw the canary that Laurenz said he owned either.

Laurenz's mother dressed him in ridiculously conservative clothes, preferably with a child's necktie.

And one time a middle-aged man molested him in a park restroom. As a result, there was a briefing in kindergarten so that nothing of the sort would happen to us. Part of the briefing was a description of what had happened, narrated by Laurenz himself. He told us how this man had approached him, said that he wanted to show him something in the bathroom, and taken him by the hand, at which point Laurenz used a judo grip to toss the man into the air, swing him back and forth, and eventually hurl him into a garbage can. The kindergarten teacher asked him if he was entirely sure that things had happened in exactly this way. Laurenz said yes.

So it was unavoidable that my pleasure in chitchatting with Laurenz receded and a certain silence came over me, one which has not subsided to this day. The spoken word has been branded on my mind as something that can potentially, when availed of to an exaggerated extent, turn out dangerous, or inconsistent, in the sense of: withdrawing from reality and/or altering its shape.

I can't escape the feeling that the visitor is keeping himself alive by eating my socks. I therefore inform him that I am considering acquiring new fish and he will in consequence, if he doesn't leave the fish alone, be furnished with a new muzzle.

I sometimes forget that outside exists, snuggles up against the house, and wants to be appreciated. All that exists for me is an inside, and in that inside there is nothing but the visitor, who used to be so small and manageable and whose extremities are now so big that they fill all ten rooms of my house. He's grown so fast that for a long time now he's had to duck his head when he walks through a door, and I'm constantly tripping over parts of his body.

I can't help but gasp and wheeze when I think about how, when I'm trying to log his scurrilous behavior, the visitor stands behind me, with a book (clearly just a mockup of a book), and peeks over at my page as soon as I start writing. I immediately cover the paper with my hands, forearms, and elbows—I lean across the whole table so that my swim-team shoulders will hide the paper's top-secret contents—no more than the tips of my toes connect me to the ground—and yet I know perfectly well that his peeking, plus his sudden bodily size, have already given him access. He has seen everything, read everything, figured everything out. The rulebook, the winter, the visitor's hairs, and first and foremost his body all continue to get longer and longer, but the argument connected to these facts has long since slipped my mind.

Even as a child I ran a well-equipped detective office, up in the attic. From it I investigated cases such as: Who unscrewed my unicycle pedal? In this mysterious case, suspicion quickly fell upon Laurenz's mother: the footprints in the grass more or less matched her shoe size, etc. Unfortunately, despite this, it was not possible to prove her guilt, and anyway I lost all interest in unicycles soon afterwards, and also in detective work. I even had to drop out of detective camp in Meiringen, which I had signed up for, due to homesickness. My parents reluctantly came to fetch me.

Now laughter rings out in the distance, but I couldn't say where it's coming from. I constantly have the feeling that things can't be found where one thinks they're to be found. I am not a good detective. And today I'm really not feeling well. When I dare to look out the window, a frosted-glass light has descended upon the scenery. The sky appears overcast, with a narrow sunbeam surmisable only in the farthest reaches of a valley located behind the lake. The mountain sometimes looks so lovely that it's unendurable. The mist at its feet, or foothills—the evening mood—the reddish sun. I've never actually wanted the view to be so charming. I never wanted it to make my heart swell and shoot blood and warmth through my body. I've always wanted to be a stone, like the mountain.

I'm writing another letter, or, to be specific, a condolence letter to a woman whose husband recently died all too young, and I imagine that this will be the last sign of life from me.

What does the guy with the sunglasses outside my house actually want?

From time to time my gaze through the binoculars roams across his monochromatic skin coloration, tattoos, and head hair. Sometimes I imagine the drawings detaching from his upper body and scrambling over mine. Then I slide via binocular view up to his head.

Should the visitor ever happen to be swept away from here the way the dirt is swept from the street by the rain, I would watch him float off, his body bobbing in the waves. Maybe I'd wave. Maybe I'd cheer, although I've gotten out of the habit of cheering and wouldn't much like the visitor to get me back into it.

Before the naked visitor can shut the door, I turn the binoculars around and now see him leave as a faraway figure. When you turn binoculars around you quickly come to survey a whole property, a whole plot of your land. When you look through binoculars the right way you can only see pathetic little snippets of something much larger, but reversed binoculars let you play the major landowner. I let my gaze rove across my estates, the model railroad, the tiny mountain shrunk down to the size of a souvenir, the Roundel Bar. It's so easy to possess something small, I think as I lower my binoculars.

Maybe I should get myself some children.

When the visitor is gone temporarily, I plummet into time. His bed is empty. The vacuum cleaner nozzles twitch helplessly. I have never once up until now thought of installing a camera in his room, but I could change my mind about that. There's a dishwasher to empty, there's a blanket to shake straight, he should read more to me from the book.

With my binoculars I finally discover him in the Roundel Bar. He's easy to recognize; he's holding a glass in his brushfingers and taking a sip from it every now and then. His face is shining as people more or less surround him. I find myself once again reminded of the well-known sect leader, my great-grandfather, who brandished skillfully spontaneous sermons and enjoyed great esteem. Even the Roundel's gold wall decals flutter at the visitor. While normally everyone at the bar sits at their respective point of the circumference, brooding away on their own, now everyone's crowding into the visitor's side of the circle, like a bunch of human grapes. The visitor is gesticulating wildly, showing his pointy teeth—he seems so fully in his element. Even the waiter looks almost friendly.

With my back on the sofa's armrest, I imagine it as the wall of a sarcophagus; I'm trapped inside it, true, but still it's a perfectly adequate enclosure for me. I just can't do it, "it" being keep this house, the many rooms and the yard, under control. I traverse these rooms every day with my body, yet never fully inhabit them. I wonder if my parents would be disappointed if they knew how unsatisfactorily I occupy their house. The crates standing around, and the visitor, must at all costs be prevented from abandoning this empty void.

Day is already dawning, some birds or other are shrieking mercilessly through the yard, the mountain is framed in yellow since the sun behind it is just waiting to leap out and turn the night into a garishly dazzling situation.

At some point I must have fallen asleep on the sofa, which I've pushed over to the window so that I could have the best possible view of the visitor. One of the binoculars' lenses is broken, so abruptly did I nod off on it. Now when I want to look at the Roundel Bar through it, first of all there's no one there and second of all there's a crack in my field of vision.

If someone were to ask me whether I'd rather oppress or be oppressed, I would invariably choose the former. I want to dominate, but am doomed to a crushing defeat. My kingdom has been confiscated. My moats, as well as my thousand-man army, are unable to bring the enemy to his knees. His resistance is colossal. Even when a rain of arrows descends upon him, to the accompaniment of hellish peals of laughter, the visitor just sits on the sofa, relaxed, politely asking if I wouldn't mind changing the TV channel, he can't stand war films. I retort that this is a knight movie, and then, contrite, I change the channel to a show where people are wandering around in a foreign country.

There are places with especially silly-sounding names that I want to visit. I picture how I'd connect them to one another on the map and spend the rest of my life strolling along the lines. Or else I'd drop a toy figurine onto a world map and then travel to the place of impact. Nowadays I flip through atlases almost every day, but the bird's-eye perspective exceeds my imaginative capacities. I find it impossible to memorize the shapes of the countries—the lines are pitiful representations and I find their significance dubious. I think: This intended overview makes it impossible to grasp the eventual reality. The bird's-eye perspective— never entirely ours, since we can fly only with the help of continual mechanical efforts—is a mix of romantic dreaminess and scientific attainment, yet really it belongs only to birds.

Is that the police driving up and down the street, their vehicles' headlights lighting everything up? the visitor interrupts me. Strange sounds boom through the night. The visitor is increasingly suffering from a persecution complex.

While my right arm is covered with moles my left is empty. Normally the visitor likes to take a pen, draw lines connecting the moles, and act like he has thereby solved the riddle of the universe. And when I cut my leg hair recently, it grew back longer than ever in no time at all. I don't care, I don't have anything against leg hair.

There are people at the door, coming in across the threshold, bringing masses of alcoholic drinks, marching down into the basement, smoking in the yard and on the second floor. They're setting up dance floors everywhere, lying in my bed, jumping around, thirsting for attention by trying to kiss me and then throwing themselves onto the floor and playing dead. The visitor's so-called friends are spreading through the house like smoke bombs.

On one of the dance floors an ex-couple are holding each other tight, their faces pressed flat against each other. Someone who introduced herself to me as Carla is dancing around the red-jacketed visitor, giggling into his neck.

I am dancing in a very small radius; in fact, the dancing is barely visible from the outside, one might just as well call it standing. I apply myself directly to the gin bottle, and with every gulp I get drunker, I get soberer, I imagine I could hit someone. More and more new dancers join the people already dancing; they pour up the narrow stairs. The plaster flakes off the walls; my silk jacket shines under the moon and the disco ball.

I climb up onto the roof via clambering through the window. The ridge of mountains, too, shines like little lambs in the moonlight. The possibility of falling off the roof does exist. Down below I see the visitor and Carla sitting on the pale stones of the flowerbeds of ornamental plants.

The visitor's name repeatedly comes out of the open windows and reaches my ears as though all the noises were just combining into this one sound.

Even though I could fit in everywhere, I fit in nowhere. I could be the most loved, favorite person in the whole small town, but instead I prefer solitude. The visitor's friends aren't friends, just people hoping his exotic nature will rub off on them. I think it's Carla's style to furnish parties with bold balloons, flutter among people dressed like a bird of paradise, and throw winks and air kisses in all directions. When Carla comes into someone's life she just brushes it with her wings, while I full-on drop into their life like a stone and have a hard time getting out again—or is it the other way around, do other people drop into my life?

I think about everyone who was ever my friend and whom I've mislaid over time. There were some who belonged to the summer and who faded in the autumn, the way the cats did from this yard I'm looking down at. A few disappeared into marriages or suchlike structures, metamorphosing into sofas. Still others evaporated when the visitor came. Most I simply never call back. I never listen to their messages; I send their letters back as though I no longer lived here. My friends are ever fewer and farther between, like the visitor's hairs, which Carla is currently running her fingers through. Well, it's winter, when hairs and fingers freeze into ugly statues that not one single museum would deign to accept. I alone will take pity on them and haul this ugly cultural heritage up next to the guardian lions and enjoy the peace and quiet on this property for the rest of my life.

Now Carla's fingers are wiggling along my spine, making my eyelids involuntarily spring open. I stand up—as is expected of me; I clatter down off the roof like a stone and land in a circle of people who have made themselves warm and comfortable around a table. Carla no longer has a place to sit (as though we were playing musical chairs) and suddenly finds herself facing a kind of mini-amphitheater of expectant looks all directed at her. She says at once that she doesn't know what made her think of it but she once had neighbors who were obsessed with the idea that they were living in a cursed apartment and decided to contact an exorcist. This exorcist drove up the next day in his exorcist car and showed around diplomas to clarify his level of professional expertise. He apparently had a very interesting appearance: he was wearing a long leather coat and lizardskin shoes, and his hair was long too, and black, and he had probably put mascara around his eyes. The exorcist, insofar as Carla had been able to determine through the peephole, had ordered an immediate fumigation of the property; smoke had come out through the crack of the neighbors' door for a week. Carla continues that she'd started to get somewhat worried when she heard via the neighbors that the exorcist charged exorbitant sums for the fumigation, looting as it were their entire retirement account, but there had been no other way out, especially since the present age was so unbearable that there was no imaginable future anyway. The neighbors were now living surrounded by the incense and spiritual proverbs that the exorcist had fanned into the reverberating rooms. The exorcist had been very friendly and nice, especially once he realized that the neighbors were receptive to his methods, so he recommended various additional therapies, including dustbuster therapy. Carla says that from then on she had been able to observe the neighbors sitting across from one another on their salmon-pink sofa, dustbusters in hand, reciprocally vacuuming back and forth along one another's respective fabrics, skins, and corners of mouths. It had been nice to watch, according to Carla, but despite their modest size the dustbusters had emitted a deafening racket to the point where even she, who lived next door to them, was disturbed. She was constantly jolted awake and had, at first, the feeling that she was not within her own four walls. Anyway, the noise was torture, and she'd toyed with the idea of moving out, but she remained so fascinated by the neighbors and their exorcist that she was barely capable of leaving her apartment anymore. She found it amazing that the dustbuster therapy seemed to work. At the end of the treatment, the affected parties were less affected, or at least less afflicted by cares and sorrows than when it started. Yes, the treatment had made the neighbors indifferent. What used to make them furious had been sucked away. What had once brought them together had crumbled into dust. You couldn't deny the treatment's ninety-nine percent success, just as the exorcist had advertised on his car, Carla says, her vocal intonation now strangely altered. Everyone—including Carla herself—had been, she says, very pleased with the results, even if the building had turned into one big cloud of smoke. Everyone was constantly stumbling over things, but upbeat about it. The neighbors had signed one check after the other, but remained upbeat. The exorcist had had all the walls and floors of the neighbors' apartment torn out—the parquet, the wallpaper, and all the kitchen appliances had had to be completely stripped out. The neighbors remained stoic, there between the torn-out tiles and the knocked-down walls. They all, including Carla, respected the exorcist highly. His personality was round and self-contained, an aura entirely of one color. He never seemed to be in a bad mood, always driving up with his hair blowing silkily behind him. Aside from that, he divided people into Good People and Bad People and by doing so got through life in the best possible fashion, while everyone else had a miserable time dragging themselves from psychologist to psychologist, from pitfall to pitfall, from bad lover to even worse lover, and then felt compelled to toss down copious amounts of drugs too. The exorcist, Carla says, had a funny and playful wife. She was a muzzle manufacturer by profession. In the summer, when the exorcist set aside his leather coat and peacocked around the pool in swim trunks, you could see lots of bite wounds on his arms. He bore them with pride, exactly as though they'd been scars from victorious battles. His wife's teeth were stumps and she had a somewhat shabby but endearing office. In it were countless aquariums all piled up; whole swarms of fish gawked silently back at you, Carla goes on, her own gaze fixed on the table. Then the exorcist, from one day to the next, could no longer be reached. The neighbors were worried, and she herself had been amazed at the exorcist's disappearance, Carla says. At first everyone was inconsolable, repeatedly hoping against hope, even considering placing a missing person notice in the newspaper. The neighbors went on living in their destroyed home a little while longer, then moved to another part of town. She, Carla, kept living in the building. Only a few weeks went by before someone new, one Mr. W., rented the destroyed next-door apartment. He moved in, seemed to be single, and quiet and withdrawn in other ways as well, to the point where one hardly saw his face. She, that is Carla, nonetheless peeped through the peephole one night and despite the darkness, W.'s short blond hair, and his jeans jacket, she could ascertain that he was none other than the ex-exorcist. At that point, Carla breaks off her story and for the rest of the night doesn't take it up again.

Smoke's properties are fascinating.

Smoke has a similar effect on the visitor as laughing gas: it makes him howl with laughter. He bumps into things, stumbles around, but is upbeat. He fans clouds of smoke around, grinning; he makes temporary sculptures from the smoke; but he never loses his good cheer. The visitor's sudden cheeriness is driving me crazy.

Whereas smoke almost makes me forget how to breathe, it is only in smoke that the visitor really starts to thrive. In fact, he hums a little song, which he interrupts only when another burst of laughter comes over him. When I try to join in, I have a coughing fit. Tears stream across my face but the coughing doesn't stop.

As the duration between puffs of a shared cigarette is compressed, the two mouths unavoidably approach each other along the y-axis.

Later, I try to calm down two brawling men but remain unmoved by the whole thing. Not even the prospect of a punch in the face stirs my soul. I remain as stony as the lion statues. One guy shoves another against the wall, makes a super-aggressive face, and waves threateningly over his head the iron bar that is actually a bike's torn-off kickstand. I stand right next to them, almost singing. At some point the threatener leaves the other one alone and flings the kickstand out into the snow-covered field.

By the time the police come, some of the houseguests have already cut and run, mine included. The police say the party's obviously much too loud and they're tempted to impound the stereo, but it looks heavy, so they'll turn a blind eye once again, I do come across as cooperative. Do you live alone here? the older cop asks me. Are you looking for someone? I retort.

What comes to mind is one time when there was a crime I had to help explain. The cop brought me behind a one-way mirror like I'd only ever seen in the movies. The potential criminals were led into the room we could see through the mirror. They had to line up, and in their hands they were actually holding numbers. I looked at the faces, my gaze slipping from one to the next and then back. A policewoman bent down to me and said that I should indicate a suspect only if I was entirely sure, otherwise it was better not to say anything. I was sure. I recognized him from his brown teeth, his beady little eyes like a mole's. The police-woman gave me a questioning look but I shook my head, shrugged my shoulders, and was led back out of the room.

At some point—the cops must have left a long time before—I feel the visitor put his hand on my shoulder. When I turn around, he squints his eyes to little slits because he's forgotten to put his glasses on, at which I yank the wineglass out of his hand, arguing that it's still actually my wineglass, just like it's also my shoulder, my Birkenstocks, my vacuum cleaner collection, my cat-deterrent siren, my house, my terrycloth un-derwear, and above all my red jacket. The truth is, I can't get to the end of enumerating all my many pieces of property, I don't have anywhere near enough fingers and especially not enough index fingers to point to them all. The visitor ducks as if I'm about to physically assault him. Whose is the visitor, actually?

I resolve to write my name in thick letters on each and every one of my possessions from now on.

Laughter rings out from the roof, the last bingo has been called, the very last cigarette smoked on the balcony. Somebody is asleep on the sofa under the Scottish blanket that my brother gave me for my birthday once.

My head boasts a pigtail that the visitor braided for me and that now feels hard when I lie on the pillow. The visitor whispers my name through the door. I can hear him standing outside my room thinking about whether he should come in and lie down next to me. At some point he creaks away across the parquet, goes down the stairs, and rushes out into the morning. I dream about Siberia, about gigantic exhibition halls, about lofts and walls hung with artworks. I dream about strangers' beds and my own beds, about death. When I wake up a song is playing throughout the whole house. It's called "No Surprises."

He is delighted beyond words, the head of tourism for our small town writes me, that countless people are interested in a stay here—not that that comes as a surprise to him, after all our town has incredibly much to offer. The mountain, for example, depending on how the light hits it, looks like a pyramid. My visitor, too, he writes, has turned out to be a major fan of our locale, which makes him, the head of tourism, very happy, and reminds him that this is primarily due to him and his publicity campaign. In any case, he is writing me now to point out that I might possibly not be keeping clearly in mind what distinguishes a visitor, namely, temporariness. In the event that I am not in a position to understand this concept, he writes, he will permit himself to clarify with a relevant comparison. One might picture a visitor as a sudden downpour: one stands under a shelter and waits for it to move quickly on. Since, however, he, the head of tourism, unfortunately seems to feel an unpleasant sensation creeping up over him, namely that the visitor as well as I have turned this cloudburst into a rainy season if not indeed a neverending hailstorm, he feels called upon to give me a fine (as well as a gold medal in honor of my combat against dust), which I am to pay as promptly as possible, and in addition the visitor must now finally rise up in his Birkenstocks—or whosever they are—and shuffle off.

I put down the letter. Still lying in bed, I see before my inner eye my former physics teacher shaking his hand back and forth in pain after slashing it open with a pair of pliers while conducting a physics experiment. He wrapped his wounded hand in the blackboard rag, which was soaked with blood within seconds, and went on teaching as though nothing had happened. His face pale, he wrote formulas up on the blackboard with one arm as blood dripped rhythmically onto the floor from his shredded hand. It felt like hours passed before the bell rang, letting our physics teacher leave the room and head to the teachers' lounge, where another teacher immediately called an ambulance.

I always pictured life differently.

And now the incongruence of things is epitomized and embodied for me by the visitor putting on an extremely long but extremely bad improvised lip-sync performance in his underpants, and the only way I can think of to make the gesticulating visitor stop is to point out to him that he risks looking like someone is holding an electrically charged balloon over his hair.

Let's assume the visitor was really an insect and just didn't look like one. Let's assume the visitor no longer made any moves to leave. Let's assume the visitor's hunger was insatiable. Let's assume the visitor ended up here by order of the government. Let's assume the visitor brought bedbugs into the house. Let's assume the visitor was one big traveling bedbug. Let's assume the visitor was actually somebody else. Let's assume the visitor really did secretly understand our language. Let's assume the visitor wanted to poison us. Let's assume the visitor's stench would never be gone from our upholstery, our rooms.

We set off smoke bombs without end but the bug refuses to fly away.

Crises come in waves. Earthquakes, too, come in waves and leave in their wake a world torn apart: as though these houses weren't meant to be lived in, these bridges not meant to be crossed. The crises concerning the visitor's presence slosh over me, cold and unstoppable. Just a moment ago I had been immersed in everyday life, counting the stripes on the sweater, smoothing down the bedspread, seeing the filaments of dust dangling from the ceiling, pouring tea into a glass. Then, all of a sudden: the stripes overlap like pick-up sticks, the bedspread is piled up alarmingly, the filaments of dust are a-tremble, the tea hangs in midair like a glass sculpture before splattering to the floor.

Before, this place was a home, now it's a hovel. The yard is a disaster area. The rosemary has been crushed flat, there's gravel in the flowerbeds, and strewn everywhere as though after an earthquake are beer cans, paper plates, plastic cups, slush, and halves and quarters and smaller pieces of all kinds of things—you peer out of your foxhole and you know, as well as you know anything, that you've never liked fractions.

Even the back of my head is flat in a way that forces you to suspect that someone broke a fraction of it off.

The visitor turns my close friends into passing acquaintances, turns passing acquaintances into zombies buried all around my house or sitting at the bar in the Roundel waiting for me to come along so that they can toss down one beer after another, which will come spritzing back out of their rotting putrid bodies without it in any way preventing them from laughing. They're downright shaking, and they snort down another couple of party drugs, which then run out onto the floor with the pools of beer, making a marbled pattern. Now who's going to lick that up, who's going to wipe that down? Even now the devilish waiter has a grin on his face.

The visitor says: You need to leave this house, this house belongs to your parents, it belongs to your brothers and sisters, it's not yours, and anyway you've stayed in this house much too long. Part of growing up is moving out of the house where you set cats' souls free, getting your own apartment, maybe even leaving this small town where they're trying to kill you.

The visitor often comes across like that: like he's blind but has seen everything. But wasn't that my role? Isn't it me who's seen everything even though she pretends to be blind?

I trudge through the yard, kicking little chunks of snow ahead of me. It's powdering down white, the mountain isn't even visible. I imagine the earth turning and everyone turning with it except me. People seem to accept their changes, their deterioration, their death, their decay, so easily, while I resist change so strongly I gouge grooves into the landscape like a car's brakes. Then I see cats' footprints in the snow.

As I stomp back up the little stairway between the guardian lions—giving them quick pats on the head—I see through the windowpane the back of the visitor's head, shining, as he sits at the table with two or three other figures. He seems to be having a tea party with people ominously like me. I spring backwards into the yard, like a startled cat—I almost hiss—and I race via yard and street to the Roundel, where the waiter asks me why I'm panting and wheezing so disgustingly, and all I can do in response is give a tired grunt.

I feel like Uncle Walter, who one time, when I was young, let himself be convinced to come stay with us. His German Shepherd tugged him into the house after it, where, due to the large number of people he found there, he stopped in the hall and stood, paralyzed, before turning around without another word and letting the canine beast drag him back out of the house.

Leashes give the people holding them stooped backs—or is it that people with stooped backs have the proper body shape for holding dogs?

Oh visitor, oh visitor, why do you open the gate for every nanny goat? Don't you see her wolfish claws? Oh visitor, oh visitor, haven't you realized that doors exist to be locked, to be sealed, to create a barricaded existence, an undisturbed life? That we will die, together, if you leave an opening in the circle through which they can gallop in, like wolves? Oh visitor, oh visitor, am I not enough for you, is my house not shelter enough for this world? Must you summon in death, the ending that lurks in all things, by tucking the enemy in on our sofa and feeding him cookies?

I have finally managed to install a large lock on the front door. I inherited no handyman abilities whatsoever, neither from my mother's side of the family nor from my father's, but the visitor, under my guidance, without any big protest, screwed the lock on. It's not like I'm a fearful person, but I do feel better now that any additional houseguests will stay locked out for the time being, especially since my cat-deterrent siren seems hardly able to keep a single cat from trampling the flowerbeds. I also insinuate to the visitor that he will be able to carry out his housework in a more carefree state if the building is nice and bolted shut. Plus his friends and admirers can meet up outside the house, if they need to meet up at all.

If anyone rings the bell anyway, it is advisable not to open the door. Should the visitor be inclined to hurry to the door notwithstanding, he is to be stopped straightaway by flinging oneself across his path. At that point, from one's horizontal position, one can (optionally) pull up one's sweater, thereby making any visitor immediately forget his original plan to open the door.

One should hide all the telephones, too, for the visitor's benefit.

If the vacuum cleaner nozzles would be so kind as to not always mimic everyone's singing.

I have a dream that I forget right away, lying on the soft sofa that one does now and then have to rub the wrong way, against the grain of the fur. It sucks me in, always attracting me to where it's warmest and where you can lie in a fetal position and imagine you have something resembling a life. The visitor recenters me in a domestic position, making me shudder. Even though I've never wanted to have a real home, here I am, genuinely living here.

The lamps have started flickering. The soldered wires are increasingly coming loose.

People live somewhere, they pay rent, then they sublet the place to someone, who sublets it further to someone else, and so on. It's a chain of subleases, each implying the next and suggesting that the highest goal is to own something. The subletters' subletters sit on furniture that is second-hand or third-hand or passed down through a whole chain of hands that can't even be fully traced back.

And then, in the end, the houses are usually empty, because the people living there have long since moved away, leaving behind traces of subsubsublets.

Some people collect rooms while others don't have even one room, as though it were really all that difficult to simply share your rooms a little.

It is all the more urgent that the visitor's body stays in these rooms rather than drifting around outside somewhere.

Actually I wanted to get rid of it—the vacuum cleaner collection. Actually I thought that the time had come to part from the nozzles. In the end they just get in the way, take up all the visitor's space, and wantonly snuffle at his bags. I had no way of knowing that the visitor would be capable of taming and training the vacuum cleaner nozzles lickety-split. Every so often they perform for me one of the pieces they're rehearsing together. Like synchronized swimmers they dance up and down, flap here and there, raise their trunks and trumpet out melodies. As I spectate, I droop with sadness. I can barely get up from the sofa; applauding is a great strain. I wasn't planning to cheer anyway. The vacuum cleaners bow their nozzles politely. Outside, sunlight falls unexpectedly onto the trees, whose bare limbs reach out weakly toward it, yes, practically cuddle up with the light. The mountain peak has impaled one single rain cloud, which now disgorges its contents onto the mountain. Streams come down the slopes, pick up branches and medium-sized rocks here and there, and make of them a little heap at the foot of the mountain.

Did someone ask me something? The vacuum cleaner nozzles suction gently at my hands, asking for a tasty treat, but I can't manage to stand up. Will I ever again?

The problem with my Holy Book is that it's always out of date. By the time I've finally written all the house rules down, the visitor has already broken new ones. It's very stressful that the regulations constantly need to be reworked, not least because while I'm doing so the visitor can nimbly evade my attention. But if it's my gaze that's supposed to monitor and/or constitute the visitor, he just suddenly slips free, moves somewhere else, with fluttering margins. His vanishing lives within him. He is the embodiment of simultaneity, of arriving in leaving. How can I sketch his outline when he's constantly in motion? How am I supposed to keep him in position when he's defined by dissolution? Does one need better tools to keep the visitor in check? Sharper glasses? Bigger binoculars? It's impossible to say.

Even though I rarely permit him to take the hallway that leads to the front door and thence outside, his spiritual form is spreading out to cover our small town like a blanket. Everyone seems to know about my visitor, everyone drops by my house, allegedly by chance, hoping that the visitor will be lying, lightly clothed, on the sun deck. Everyone thinks they know a thing or two about what to do with this visitor's body that now belongs to me. At least I was the first person to spot him, on the train platform back then. The visitor and I exchanged glances and sealed our fate and/or progress together through time.

Time changes arrivals, casts them in another light. The history of his arrival changes the story of my potential departure.

The small town where we live together—or really should I say: where I try to keep the visitor hidden away?—is in a remote and increasingly forsaken place. Today, when I stepped across the threshold of a restaurant where I've never in my life shown my face, one head after another turned to face me, watched me walk toward my chair, where I gracefully took a seat and gave a ghastly smile to all and sundry. After not too long, I was requested to supply my name, age, and place of origin, that is: to identify myself, or to get lost—forever. I sat there brooding over the request, hunched over a beer, lost in thought, continuing to be observed by the people all around me.

Although the language of politics is one I have always found objectionable, I had the romantic idea just then that the true essence of integration could only be for it to happen unremarked, the way a peloton of bike racers will ride up to a lead biker who has pulled ahead and so to speak swallow him up as though he were no different from them—and I shoved the smoked sausages the waiter had expectantly laid out for me, together with a couple of black olives, into my mouth.

I look for evil in the outside world but find it only within. My eyes, ringed by bags, peer out between them as little dots. The water is full of chlorine and chalk, and increasingly clogs my arteries. The chair I'm sitting in slopes, too, so that I'm constantly at risk of slipping off.

The town smells different than usual, as though it were suddenly located near a body of water where shrieking seagulls are ripping out fishes' guts. I no longer know what to say about the birds. Mostly I try to ignore them, so as not to be jealous of them.

Life is a process of conforming to what one knows. I wonder how people can help being ashamed of going around constantly repeating the same thing—the same Scandinavian backpacks, as though there were nothing else to possibly stow utensils in. When my rulebook is finished, someday, not only will the visitor be tamed but I will have at last written a true scripture, which others, too, will find extremely useful.

I flip through a book about parasites and in every example I recognize my visitor. I read that parasites—the polar opposite of lions in this regard—do not swallow their prey, they gently force their prey into a common cause: they make their own wishes the host's wishes, probably like in a marriage. It's a comfortable death. Maybe the visitor has passed over into me so thoroughly, maybe he's turned what's his into mine so long ago, that I can no longer even harbor the thought of resisting him.

The visitor has nested in me to such an extent that no matter how hard I try to rebel against him I am in the end only destroying myself.

That's the last thing I think before I fall asleep over my book about parasites—before a sleep comes over me that seems to me like it isn't mine.

I got really sick and tired of Laurenz copying everything I did. He mimicked all my actions, repeated everything I said. All my life I've been looking for a counterpart, but all I ever find is someone who plagiarizes me.

The thing about Laurenz was that he always tried to be near me, as though he felt good only when I was sheltering him from the wind. His mother felt obligated to inform my parents, over the phone, that Laurenz secretly didn't want to be my friend anymore. She said that Laurenz had made it clear that I was forcing him to spend time with me and keeping him prisoner even when he wanted to leave.

I told Laurenz: So leave.

He started following me after school, lurking in bushes, tailing me everywhere. I confronted him but he lied, he said he didn't know anything about any mother prohibiting our friendship, he'd never told anyone he didn't want to see me, his mother was making things up.

We got more and more phone calls from Laurenz's mother. My parents got tired of them and recommended that I give Laurenz up. So I did. I had myself seated at a distance from him in school; I stopped answering his love letters.

The suns go up, the suns go down, and yet I can never look right at them.

Suddenly I start finding tangerine peels in my bed. Brushfinger hairs are strewn across the floor, and the notebooks I've mentioned, in which I try to capture and understand and ward off the visitor with countless drawings and sentences, are lying around open and chewed on. The titles (*Studies in Departure; The Settlers 2; Forms of Possibility – Man As Visitor; Soft Tissue*) are now illegible. The portraits of the visitor, now covered with teeth marks, peer back at me like creepy mutations, and stuffed between the pages are the letters from the town's head of tourism, from exes, from Carla, and from my brothers and sisters.

The visitor has clearly been rummaging around in my room while I've been gone. Things reel and stagger like a single-engine plane above the Siberian forests.

He bellows my name through the house. Again and again. But I play dead.

I haven't mentioned this up until now, but there are little line drawings of animals embroidered on the Persian carpet, maybe llamas, or maybe squirrels. A human figure stands facing one of the animals with his arm reaching out toward it. There is a green object in his hand, maybe a pear, maybe a bottle of beer. The figures are too small to have faces, and they are woven into the center of the carpet, framed in a rhombus; their rigid immobility makes them seem lost.

If only I could solve the riddle of the carpet.

Today I think that the solution must have something to do with the occupation of small territories. But I'm sick of having to reduce my inquisitorial desires to such small fry, just because that's what I've been taught. I no longer want to hang around some dollhouse-like small town and light it up with little lightning-like light switches, when after all I could also unleash a storm on some bigger swath of land.

Back then I did make a drawing of Laurenz's grave—he deserved it. It was the best strategy I had: using this drawing to acknowledge, dispel, and put behind me both him and his hypocritical pretenses, or, rather, his mother's hypocritical pretenses.

Then, most unfortunately, this drawing managed via various inconvenient detours to end up in the hands of another child's parents, who were part of the campaign being waged against my bad upbringing and who made a beeline straight for Laurenz's mother to hand over the artwork. Everyone, my own parents included, was then deeply ashamed that I seemed to be capable of wishing death upon my ex-boyfriend, and as a result numerous heated discussions ensued about whether or not I should be expelled from school (I was nine by this point).

Everyone except my parents was delighted that a transgression had finally taken place which they were able to prove I had committed and which, therefore, ensured the separation forever of Laurenz and me. All the accusations concerning my spoiled nature had turned out one hundred percent justified. Laurenz's mother, too, could now with cleaner conscience suggest more advantageous influences on her son, for example Saskia, a nice horse-girl without a single amusing idea in her head and with a university-degree-holding housewife for a mother, as Laurenz's mother was too for that matter.

Since then my confidence vis-à-vis the genus Parent has never returned, something I find quite depressing. It sometimes happens, even now, that when I find myself in the presence of a parent not my own I start mumbling and become exaggeratedly polite to the point of making normal conversation impossible.

I tried to wean myself off of the impulse to honor Laurenz, i.e., to write about him, but I have been unable to refrain from looking him up on the internet. The fact that he now belongs to a not entirely unknown religious sect, and seems to have married within it, comes as no great surprise. More mesmerizing to me are his pictures, which show him admittedly happy, that is to say: smiling, but always in the same pose, his head tilted twenty degrees to the left, the eyes in his head stabbing sharply into me from behind his gold-rimmed glasses. So I click through this Laurenzian statuary until I come across the one photo with no people in it at all: slightly blurry, the scene spookily illuminated by the flash, it shows a plate full of edible penguins, assembled as if in a game of Exquisite Corpse from carrots (feet and nose), crème fraîche (belly), and olives (arms and head), perhaps held together with a vertical toothpick. No one has commented on or liked this picture.

I think it wasn't entirely outside the realm of possibility that things could have worked out well. It must have been years later that I saw Laurenz sweeping up garbage on the street and concluded that either he had a trainee position with the sanitation department or a summer job with ditto. One could see it in his delicate limbs, his swollen eyes. And when I think about it today, I reach the conclusion that it looked like he was not completely convinced that it was a good idea to be born into this world. I have been perpetually and, as it were, magically attracted to this existential quandary, I now think, especially because I considered myself fully in a position to answer it with my presence.

I act like I don't care when I first see Laurenz's mother's death notice in the newspaper, but later I feel the morbid longing to go look for her grave.

I saw a scene on TV with people dancing while carrying a coffin. It reminded me that at my grandmother's funeral a gigantic painting of an angel was hanging above the minister's lectern. As I examined it, a fit of laughter suddenly came over me, which I tried to suppress by pressing both hands to my face; tears welled out from beneath them, ran over my mouth and chin, and dripped onto the stone church floor. When the minister left the pulpit after his speech and the lute player started up again, I couldn't think of anything else to do besides jump up and hurry out of the church, still convulsing.

I've always had a thing for the terminology around people's extermination. I think *Inside a Murderer* but think it idly. I think about two ways to kill someone: secretly mix ground glass into their food, or write stories about them, freezing their life in notation.

I also remember again the fish graves out in the yard, and the little crosses that I decided to put up despite not being religious. The tiny nameplates I affixed to the graves: Hugo, Hugo Two, Huga, Leonora.

I think of an exhibition where you were supposed to lie down on war victims' graves wearing socks and transparent raincoats. An audio recording played from inside the ground, narrating the death of the deceased man or woman while you yourself lay on an empty bag of potting soil in the warm gallery room.

My father once announced that when he died he didn't want a grave of his own. He pictured instead an anonymous mass grave, between trees for instance, and he insisted that his name not be displayed anywhere. Not long thereafter, my parents decided that they no longer considered themselves able to fill this house, where they lived, and where the visitor and I now live (or have we already melted together into a single body?). They said they would rather take up less space than they hitherto had, and they stroked my magnificent hair. Then they moved into a smaller apartment, far from everyone, far from me. My parents shrunk a little every day and made no effort whatsoever to combat it. I can't forgive them for that.

Now it's not thirst that I suddenly feel and that lures me away from the table—it's my doubts about the truth content of my paraphrasings. Words seem to descend into my mind from the void, which I then recite to others, uncertain but willing to go along with it—let's put it this way: like Power Point karaoke—but the words nonetheless sometimes feel like they aren't mine.

Is that the distant singing of the vacuum cleaner nozzles I hear, or is it the wind?

The waiter asks where the visitor's been recently. What visitor? I ask.

The waiter says that he used to work in a hotel, which was shaped like a mountain and painted bright yellow, he had no idea who could have designed such hideous architecture. Well, visitors seldom turned up at this hotel-mountain—now and then a stray, lone individual would drift into the lobby. Only rarely did a whole bus full of international travelers drive up. He says he'd had a lot of time to think about things when he worked at the hotel-mountain, sometimes in the restaurant, sometimes cleaning. For example, he decided to become rich, and realized at the same time, he goes on, why he so liked his job. It was because even though he always had to act extremely polite and helpful, he could feel completely superior to the guests on the inside. They made it, so to speak, easier for him to perceive his own contours and/or magnitude. To him the guests were like guardrails, but very curved ones, and it was precisely these curves that made him so straight, he says, plus he had finally been able to buy an expensive vacation home, which he rented out in turn. Life without visitors had become unthinkable to him. So anyway, he says, if I ever felt like a vacation he could recommend this property highly. In fact, he would even consider offering it at a special bargain price for friends, in my case.

The waiter stares at me with his greedy eyes. I am, he says he just noticed, an elegant woman, that is to say, my face is nothing special, almost boring really, almost a little arrogant, but he means that as a great compliment. At this point someone else at the bar jumps in and says I really am beautiful, that is: *Jolie, n'est-ce pas?* The waiter cries *Non!* and puts another beer in front of me, my seventh. They serve them in skinny little glasses called *Herrgöttli* and you can drink them endlessly.

Just look at how he walks right through the door now, without knocking. Just look at him scrabbling across the parquet floors toward me. Just look at how his brushfingers stroke the windowpanes, as though he's a prisoner in this house, gazing out at a freedom closed off to him. Just look at how the visitor scratches at the glass, even. He looks at me, questioningly, so questioningly, and I say: I don't know either. I pet him, tugging his eyes, forehead, and folds of face skin toward the back of his head. His head lies in my hand, streamlined tight.

The woman in the light-gray coat, probably still without any fixed place of residence, is standing outside my house and seems to have all the time in the world to look at my walls, let her eyes wander, study one window after the other, including the paint flaking off the frames. Her gaze lingers on the window behind which I'm standing, looking out.

On the radio there's a report about the allure of the newly arisen antifascist movements, another dissecting Islam, another about poets who write about flowers, another about cravats becoming fashionable again. A strange feeling creeps up over me: that I've missed out on more than I wanted to, as though the whole news broadcast is under the control of a totalitarian state that has seized power without my realizing it. The walls of this house have grown so thick, the people living inside it so thin. When I look outside, I can't tell if it's still the same winter as yesterday or if it's already the next one. Sometimes I can't even tell the difference between day and night, between dream and whatever the other thing is, I have no idea what to call it. I think I'm sometimes the only person who hears this sound—a quiet sound, resting on and around things, making me tilt my head, like a slow tracking shot, all gentle and fading. Sometimes I decide to die, and then I don't know what I mean by that.

Laurenz always told me things are supposed to change, but maybe he didn't say that at all, maybe I'm just imagining us as old even though we only knew each other when we were young and understood nothing, but actually understood everything. I don't miss those days. I don't miss the world saying I'm too little to understand even though it was always the world that was too little.

When a visitor wants to leave, that is a welcome development. When a visitor—finally!—wants to move on, one can only sign, stamp, and seal his application for departure as promptly as possible. When a visitor heads toward the door with plastic bags packed, a couple of vacuum cleaner nozzles sticking cheekily up out of them—when he heads, that is, toward where his destiny has always lain—it is not in this case necessary to stand in his way. When a visitor tries to hug me goodbye, presses his furry body against mine, wishes me all the best for the future, there is no reason at all to burst into tears: would my eyes be so kind as to snort said tears back up into them? When a visitor needs to go back where he came from, or, perchance, wants to move on to his next house, his next mistress, we must enable him to do so by letting him pass, which is to say: by taking a step to one side.

When, however, a visitor without whom the universal equilibrium and house itself will utterly collapse decides to leave, it is certainly worth entertaining the idea of stopping him. And when such a guest attempts to turn the door handle, it is at all events appropriate to yank his brush-finger away from the handle, in the direction opposite to the joint, so that he screams in pain and shock. When a visitor one has found oneself obliged to decide to forcibly keep in place tries to cut loose, it is necessary to cling to him. When one is clinging to a visitor and his plastic bags, one must not allow oneself to be shaken off—rodeo experience is desirable. When a visitor one is clinging to is the wildest horse of all, one must accept that, first, one is not even close to world-champion level when it comes to rodeo riding, and, second, one is flying toward a floor that one is about to smash into. When doors thunderingly slam shut, it sometimes happens that the panes of glass set in them burst out; (a) they head in the direction of the floor as well, and (b) the house turns into something like a paper cutout.

The new fish in the aquarium are swimming in the waters of death, suspecting nothing; they snap their teeny-tiny mouths open and shut, barely perceptibly. Are they still alive or already dead? Impossible to tell. I scatter flakes of fish food onto the surface of the water, and they sink down onto the fish like a rain of ashes, but the fish don't move an inch.

I've always had a particular thing for smashing windows. I shattered my first pane when I was just eight. The reason was a simple one. At the time I used to resist submitting to bodily cleansing, as a general rule, and thus would spend weeks at a time roaming around unshowered. Dirt stuck in my hair, under my nails—after all, I liked holding earthworms in Laurenz's face.

It goes without saying that this put me, every time, into conflict with my parents, who nonetheless tried to convince me to take a bath every two weeks. One time, my mother totally lost it—I know someone who would say that she *blew her top*—and dunked me forcibly, complete with leggings, into the half-full bathtub as I kicked and screamed. Then she carried me wet out into the hall, put me down, and locked herself back in the bathroom. I consequently beat against the door and/or its glass. I remember the short moment of surprise when the glass gave way beneath my fists. Surprise at realizing that I had always overestimated the constancy of reality, and I had absolutely been able to split it apart.

My arm was then hurriedly wrapped in a terrycloth towel and my father drove us to the hospital. They needed thirteen stitches to sew up the three slash wounds in my forearm. My parents had to wait in the hospital corridor because people wanted to ask me about how the whole thing had happened without anyone else there.

At home, my brother was meanwhile trying to vacuum the blood out of the wall-to-wall carpeting, and my sister up in the attic had decided to smash the TV set with a hammer and political zeal, since she considered its bad influence responsible for the situation. If I remember correctly, my father had tears in his eyes when we came home that night—after I had been sewn back up and bandaged—and he found the fragments of the black-and-white TV, an heirloom.

The visitor only slowly moves away from the front door. His plastic bags hang from his arms, unmotivated, pulling him down toward the ground without any contribution from me. He stands in front of the house for a while, observing the passersby. It flashes through my head that I could call someone on the phone and ask for help.

At some point I step outside the front door that now has a hole in it, even though the visitor has already shuffled off in the direction of the bus stop. I see his figure getting smaller and smaller and suddenly break into a run. I have always loved running, especially when there's no reason to. Now I see the bus pull up, stop; I see its doors open and the visitor and his plastic bags disappear inside it. When I come wheezing up, the doors are already swinging shut, so we briefly stare at each other through the door's windows. The visitor tries to operate the door opener, in vain; I see his mouth shape some words, but the bus no longer allows its doors to open, it just jerkily drives off. I see the visitor rush up to the front, to the driver, but she only shakes her head. And so they race around the corner and thenceforth they have vanished from my field of vision.

Once I get back to the place where our house once was, I sit among the rubble, among the remnants of the sad partygoers, the opened but unfinished beers, the cigarette stubs, confetti, and neon tubes. When I shout up the stairs I receive no reply; when I stare out into the garden, all I see is the dead rosemary bush that the visitor once dug up out of another garden and tried to transplant into my garden, without success. Plus a couple of broken tiles fallen from the roof.

Furthermore, I don't know who invited to the party the artist who painted an airbrush portrait of me, unasked. The painting is still leaning against the wall; the eyes that are supposedly an imitation of mine just squint uncertainly at me. The person in the picture doesn't look a thing like me but strongly reminds me of someone who actually exists. With the best will in the world, I can't think of who.

A report comes on the radio saying that somewhere in the world a bus has crashed into a wall at high speed.

Or else it's all much worse and I personally, with my very own hands, helped the visitor carry the plastic bags out of the house, stacked them nice and neat in the trunk of the taxi that drove up, vigorously slammed the trunk shut, let the visitor get in the taxi, merely raised my hand in a short farewell when the car started moving, and then turned around, walked back to the house with no visible hesitation, and lay down on the sofa, where I ate a big plate of spaghetti al limone while a show about a baby moose breaking its leg played on the TV.

At some point, my siblings will walk through the door and sweep me off the sofa and out of the house. I will roll down the little front steps, right into the cat-deterrent siren, which, despite my now not exactly youthful age, will whistle through my ear canal, and all I'll be able to do is groan along with it, four octaves lower. I will come to a stop lying on the fish graves, will look like a fish myself because the snow has melted and turned into a pond around me. I will swim in this pond and be afraid of the ghost-cats, who are all dead, admittedly, but who nonetheless try to fish for me in the pond at night with their white paws. The aquarium fish, too, will rise back up out of their graves and race me through the water. The blackest of the fish will always win, because he was my favorite. My nieces and nephews will tumble through the garden, doing gymnastics, turning cartwheels. Finally, finally, the peak will fall off the mountain and plunge right through the middle of the Roundel Bar, right onto the evil waiter staring stupidly, slack-jawed, idiotic as the moon, wanting to snatch up his meager tips but no longer able to. The remaining visitors to the Roundel will sit unscathed around the slain waiter. One woman will slip off a barstool and slowly walk toward the cash register, open it, and take out the money. The money will be divided evenly among the guests, with each one getting a couple of banknotes, a couple of coins. Someone tries to pour himself another beer from the tap, but the beer line, too, has been broken by the plummeting mountain peak. The guests now leave the bar, with their banknotes. Some settle down under the canopies, a few head toward the nearest pub at the other end of the small town and occupy it. That is, just sit at the enemies' tables until they either rush out the door or forget their enmity. Two are already clinking beer glasses. Spring is here. The furniture store, alas, is going out of business, because all the sofas have metamorphosed back into people, but the town's head of tourism is promoted to mayor, because tourists are pouring in from all sides to stare in amazement at the broken-off mountain.

This morning I yank open the front door but no one's lying there. All I see are the fish graves, a mess now, as though a desecrator has had a go at them: the little crosses made of matches are lying flat on the ground; the lilies of the valley that have crept up out of the ground unsolicited hang their heads. Quite a lot of time must have gone by. The sun shines, rather confidently considering that it's showing its face for the first time in weeks.

The "Missing" posters I put up on all the streetlamps have by and large gone unnoticed, and/or one or two people from the neighborhood call me and claim to have seen him, for instance in the village store, or, no, it was in the dance club, i.e., the Roundel Bar, but he can't have been in the Roundel Bar, I then think, because I've been in the Roundel Bar every day, imagining him coming through the door and shaking his long beautiful hair, which by now must reach the ground he's dragging it on.

I take big steps over the puddles. A black cat wants to cross the street too but reconsiders given the approaching traffic. A beige sofa sits on the sidewalk, free, as a cardboard sign corroborates. I've stored the rest of the furniture in a basement. The dressers sheathed in plastic, wrapped-up kitchen utensils, bags of clothes, crates of books. I think: the things will get bored in the basement, but then I think: the things don't care whether I use them or not. They don't need me and never have.

I mount a cityshare electric Vespa and ride out of the small town, which I know but enjoy being unfair to because I've resided there—let's say *lived*, let's say *grown up*, yes, we've grown together—too long to respect it. The sun tries to peek through the clouds but can't do it. There's a statue of a chimpanzee at the gas station, and a woman sitting in front of the statue, and she looks strangely like the chimpanzee. At the bar I pass, the usuals are leaning against the bar drinking the usual.

Once I get to the train station, I walk alongside the train and stare into the windows and the passengers' faces. I stop and linger at one. The man's eyeballs revolve calmly in sync with me. And right before he leaves my field of vision, he smiles a little, more to himself than to me.

The train rolls through a wall of fog. I imagine that out of eyeshot there's no world anymore: from now on, the world has limits. Then it occurs to me that the world really does have limits.

The man across from me never stops eating. Every few minutes he takes another container out of his suitcase, and each one contains some prepared edible—corners of sandwiches on brown toast, filling unknown, or grapefruit sliced, filleted. Everyone else in the train compartment is sleeping. After this man makes an unpleasant impression on me for seven straight hours—constantly eating, breathing loud, coughing repeatedly, taking a snort of asthma spray every so often, crinkling around in his bags, letting his cellphone ring for minutes on end—I start to like him and/or integrate him into my environment. Then I can't even imagine continuing my trip without him.

The line I have to stand and wait in turns back on itself numerous times, so I repeatedly encounter the same people. They and I give each other burning looks. The plane's late. The gates for Pristina and Istanbul have just now opened, so herds of people slowly pour out from them. It's only my herd that remains behind its barriers, pawing at the ground. It's the most beautiful weather in the world outside. The planes' tails look like shark fins, and the planes stretch them in the sun.

The small town—my refuge, my home, now just a mass of ruins—is down below me somewhere. Soccer fields shine greenly up at me. Two people next to me, who I'd thought were mother and son, are kissing. I look like a rock star, my hair hanging down over my windbreaker in a stringy mane.

I have gone my whole life without thinking about what I want to see in the world. People always told me that it is our human destiny to travel, and I did always want to move from place to place, but at the same time I could never endure having everything be either preparations for or follow-ups to a departure. What I mean is, when you're finally with someone for once, it has limits, the same way everything has limits— you know the music is about to stop, the sounds about to die out, it's about to be quitting time or midnight or the end of the month, you're about to be back at the airport or shutting the door behind you somewhere or waving as someone or another leaves, then turning around, running across the cobblestones, and traversing further locations.

What I'd like best, I now think, is if I could distribute my things and myself among as many places as possible.

The sand is gritty and coarse. Two guys are trying to surf on teeny-tiny waves with teeny-tiny surfboards, and they whistle at me, like children who can't do anything without their parents watching. I briefly look up from my book every now and then and see them miss the tiny waves because they're waving at me. A butterfly colored a poisonous green lands on my towel. The teeny-tiny waves turn into small waves, but even these don't manage to swallow up the two guys or at least carry them away. All they carry off is the beachball, at least they carry it five or ten feet. It comes to rest in a concavity. Sometimes a rip appears in the cloud cover. I don't move anymore for the time being. The baby ducks squeak around on the water, their feet absurdly long compared to their fluffy bodies. Now there are swallows too: it's a miracle they don't crash into one another as they all plunge down at the same swarm of gnats from different directions.

A seagull picks for washed-up mussels on the sand. Up the hill is the highway, with traffic thundering by—each vehicle bigger than the last. I reflect upon whether the surfer with the Turkish board has dismounted elegantly or not. I try to take the waves as they come, but they are cold and never-ending, they are unfriendly contemporaries I can't figure out how to jump over. I dive through the walls of the waves headfirst and tumble dizzily onto the sand. The surf school students sit on their boards in wetsuits. Sometimes one of them tries to shout something to another one, but the wind carries their words away and shatters them on the surface of the water. Children teeter past, collecting rocks and scrapes.

My leg hairs glow brightly with crusted-on salt; my toenails start to turn blue; the gulls just keep picking away as if they don't notice that the waves flowing back into the ocean are sucking away the sand beneath their feet. I am impenient despite approaching the desert. Another kind of bird is nesting in the bushes, and it sounds like a whimpering baby.

The next day, I lie in bed and remember how the visitor, my visitor, once told me that he'd dreamt I collapsed at the bottom of an escalator in a train station. People had had to call a rescue team, and then they stopped into the station café. I was questioned. It wasn't clear where I had arrived from, but I did have a large suitcase with me. I was apparently exhausted—probably my suitcase was full of work I hadn't done yet. So I sat with the EMTs in the café, but someone else at the next table was rustling and crinkling so loudly that we told them they had to leave.

Something is lying on the floor of the room: it looks like a crushed bug, but I refuse to pursue my speculations. I just lie there with a burning sensation inside me. For a moment I think a circling helicopter is caught in the bathroom vent.

A woman I know only in passing says later, over dinner with the consul, that every corner and edge of this country is crumbling. As though yesterday's promises were the same as today's. It's only a matter of time, she says, before everything falls apart. I fiddle with my nametag.

Then the nation's wine is served and the consul stands up to introduce it with a few words and a patriarchal sweep of his arm. The consul says he has always felt very welcome and comfortable here, even if the people remain closed off. He has never been sure if they were saying Yes or No. He has never known whether it was time to go or whether, instead, he might, or indeed must, stay a while. Moreover, they have never liked it when people were too serious—they much preferred it when people incessantly smiled. Nevertheless, he had, he says, found a temporary home here, and was thus truly sad that he now had to accept a new posting in a bigger city. It would be nice there too, to be sure, he was certain of that, perhaps even nicer—here the consul breaks off.

Everyone toasts one another. I think: I'm traveling but I can't get away.

The consul doesn't smile when he lets himself drop into the chair next to mine, and I pull my black blouse a little tighter around my shoulders. For a second I'm worried he's going to say something about my appearance but instead he looks me up and down in silence. He has noticed only recently, he goes on after a short pause, in a voice only I can hear, that our national language is a strange one in that it doesn't make us feel like we belong, wherever we are. Of course we do learn the so-called High language, but this isn't really one's own, he goes on. One might even say that we are a people, he says, putting "people" in quotes with his fingers, with only a spoken language, barely transcribable, at our disposal, therefore lacking a piece of our history. He noticed this once again, he says, when he wanted to say loving things to his now wife, who was from an Eastern European country. He had no linguistic intimacy available to him except in his dialect, which the wife, and others, even his own countrymen and -women, couldn't understand. It was comprehensible only to people from the little place where he was born and raised.

The consul looks at me, his gaze resting on me a moment too long, so that I feel forced to say something in response.

I say that "little" is a good word for it, at which the consul gives a polite smile, so I go on. I tell him that I once used to be excited about little things, but since then I've increasingly had the feeling that something was wrong with them. In our country, I say, people typically try to take up little space, not in terms of living space, there if anything the opposite is true, but with respect to their personality. In general I would sometimes forget my gender but then be reminded of it in the most brutal way since it halves the already small space I'm allotted. But maybe that's not the point here. Maybe the point is that this smallness is fake, like the terrycloth towel pressed into squares that are too small and that then, when water touches it, swells up gigantic—if you understand what I mean, I say. The consul gives me a friendly look.

I am diplomatic, but my glass keeps getting refilled with the nation's wine, which I pointedly toss down, though without enjoying it. I conclude my speech by declaring that I'm traveling to see my parents, who instructed me in smallness and subsequently skipped town.

The other women touch the food with their forks without bringing it to their mouths, and so a veritable army of smoked salmon returns to the kitchen. The pieces of salmon lie there sadly on their beds of spinach, having accomplished nothing. I say *fork* in English but I mean *knife*. An artist couple gives me a bland smile, taking little sips from their nearly empty glasses. The woman looks at her daughter as if she were the strangest creature in the world, and talks to her quietly, pleadingly, before placing her into someone else's arms.

In the well-tended embassy garden, a waitress tells me in English: There's no smoking allowed here. Please go somewhere else, as far away as possible. I go away, down the stairs, and in fact to the other end of the courtyard; there's no farther I can go. With my face to the wall, I light a cigarette and think back to him, how he kept nimbly shifting back and forth between languages as though simply touching different piano keys that combined into a frothy melody, while my language is like a ball and chain on my feet, making me an awkward person. I decide to learn his *langue principale*. I will run down the street for miles on end, conjugating at every step, my gaze slipping across things and naming them all.

Tortes are brought in; they look like plastic. Shots are brought in, presumably tequila, that we drink in one gulp, while beyond the garden the skyscrapers stand around strangely mute in the moonlight. A hand made of ice is lying in the drain. The consul puts his hand on my shoulder and asks why I'm dressed like a detective. We laugh and look down at my beige linen coat, whose collar I've flipped up. Then he says he misses the little country, and I say I miss my parents. And then we stand there.

When, not long after that, I try to slip away from the event, an embassy guard keeps me for an hour. I sit in a small room, drunk, as he demonstratively pages through my passport.

The city is one big hubbub of car horns, it is covered in a layer of dust, and dust settles onto me too. The water coming out of the shower is either very hot or very cold. Later, when I'm lying in bed, I can still see camels' feet sitting gingerly on the sand like little pillows. It's like channel-surfing through TV stations: images appear, now hackneyed, now astonishing, going by too fast for me to understand what they mean. They simply fly right through me.

Waking up is no fun. The sea's bay meanders through the landscape like a snake. The weather is relentless—either the sun blazes or the rain patters onto my skull. The sea snake just lies there, waiting it out for better times. The pool-landscape is like a prison, walled in with bars. Next to the pool is a kind of mini-pool of hot water, with people lying in it like newts. They gawk at me; the clouds sketch their shadows across the desert land. There are many things in life I have failed to understand, and what I understand the least are perhaps thong bikinis.

There's a girl in the elevator; her T-shirt shows a popsicle on a stick with a bite taken out of it, and her hand is holding a little stick with a white balloon dangling from the end. The elevator moves vertically downward—the same direction in which sadness is moving into me. The desolation in the breakfast hall . . . the circling around the coffee machines . . . the servers, always these servers.

The lobsters sit in their tanks with claws tied shut and wait for death, not knowing that they're waiting for death. I walk over to them and the look they give me cloaks me in strange humility. I know that the lobsters can be ordered from the menu in the evening. One day I too will liberate at least one of them this way.

I remember a hotel where every seat broke, folded up, shattered, or simply toppled over when sat on, like a badly made stage set. I felt at the time, and still feel, a certain sympathy for those chairs, because they refused to bear people, yes, refused their function altogether.

I eat a tartufo stracciatella. I'm the last tourist. I don't care where I go next. My fingernails get longer and longer. I could keep traveling for so long that all my temporary housing would increasingly blur together, float away.

The trucks on the desert highway make a sordid impression. Some are stranded on the side of the road like whales, and for the first time in a long time I am somewhere that doesn't seem familiar. The octopus-like cacti, the quick-footed desert hares, the little quail with its rakish hairdo. Pickup trucks drive past us—white ones and black ones in turn. I am not at all sure that the human eye was made to grasp landscapes racing by outside windows.

Everybody overtakes us and, quick as a flash, they are just a little point on the road running straight ahead for another forty miles. A black and green mountain range rises up from the plains, looking like 3D animation. The country is a patchwork quilt. Boulevards of trees are the seams between the various sewn-together parts. The thought of the mass of people who exist presses me even farther down into my seat. I've read that this is a place of extremes, and I wonder whether I am a person of extremes and whether being a person of extremes is something to aspire to.

An unforeseen cheerfulness comes over me when a boy throws up in the bus. A sweetish stench spreads throughout the vehicle, putting everyone in it into a docile mood. The stench covers our communal fate like a bell jar. The boy is swaying between the seats, his eyes rolling. The driver never stops bellowing at us passengers in a language I can't understand, yanking the steering wheel left and right in turn. Some of the occupants of the bus fall asleep, shut their eyes, because they don't want to see what there is to see.

At some point, we arrive at a city. Prefab cement buildings stacked up on both sides of the street. One person after the other is spit out of the bus and shuffles off, pressed into the ground by their luggage. Other than that, I see hardly any people outside, as if this city weren't intended to be lived in. We keep driving, the sun goes down, the streets get darker, I am the last person to heave their luggage out of the baggage compartment.

ACKNOWLEDGMENTS

I would like to thank for their support: Philippe Karrer, Jacob Teich, Venus Ryter, Moïra Gilliéron, Zino Wey, Sarina Scheidegger, Esther Ludwig-Koch, René Koch, Philipp Koch, Anna Bertrand, Aeneas Koch, Martina Koch, Fabian Grossenbacher, Johanna Koch, Julian Koch, Nora Zumbühl, Mireille Neuhaus, and Francisco Sierra, as well as Heinze Helle, Stefan Humbel, Arno Renken, Thomas Strässle, Ingo Niermann, and Lukas Bärfuss, plus the interviewers Ariane Tinner, David Kunz, and Reingard Dirscherl. Thanks too to Sunshine Ranch and its former residents.

Work on this book was supported by the Literatur Basel committee, the Swiss cultural foundation Pro Helvetia, the Swiss National Foundation for Culture, the Atelier Mondial, the Sasso Residency, and the Master of Contemporary Arts Practice department at the Hochschule der Künste, Bern.

ARIANE KOCH was born in Basel and studied fine arts and interdisciplinarity. She writes—often in collaboration—theater and performance texts, radio plays, and prose. Her texts have won numerous awards and have been performed in places like Basel, Berlin, Cairo, Istanbul, and Moscow. *Overstaying* is her debut novel.

DAMION SEARLS has translated sixty books of literature and philosophy from German, Norwegian, French, and Dutch, including the novels of Jon Fosse, winner of the 2023 Nobel Prize for Literature. His own writing includes fiction, poetry, a biography of the creator of the Rorschach test, and *The Philosophy of Translation*.